"How did you find

He looked at her from between narrowed lids. "When your father failed to do so in five years of searching?" he taunted.

"If that's how long he looked, yes."

Ethan grimaced. "We really should go somewhere more private to discuss this, Mia."

Her mouth thinned. "I said no."

Irritation darkened his brow. "We *are* going to talk, Mia."

"Whether I like it or not?"

"Yes."

All about the author...
Carole Mortimer

CAROLE MORTIMER is one of Harlequin's most popular and prolific authors. Since her first novel was published in 1979, this British writer has shown no signs of slowing her pace. In fact, she has published more than 135 novels!

Her strong, traditional romances, with their distinctive style, brilliantly developed characters and romantic plot twists, have earned her an enthusiastic audience worldwide.

Carole was born in an English village that she claims was so small that "if you blinked as you drove through it you could miss seeing it completely!" She adds that her parents still live in the house where she first came into the world, and her two brothers live very close by.

Carole's early ambition to become a nurse came to an abrupt end after only one year of training, due to a weakness in her back, suffered as the aftermath of a fall. Instead she went on to work in the computer department of a well-known stationery company.

During her time there, Carole made her first attempt at writing a novel for Harlequin Books. "The manuscript was far too short and the plotline not up to standard, so I naturally received a rejection slip," she says. "Not taking rejection well, I went off in a sulk for two years before deciding to have another go." Her second manuscript was accepted, beginning a long and fruitful career. She says she has enjoyed every moment of it.

Carole lives "in a most beautiful part of Britain" with her husband and children.

Other titles by Carole Mortimer available in ebook:

Harlequin Presents

2994—TAMING THE LAST ST. CLAIRE*
2988—THE RELUCTANT DUKE*
2982—THE RETURN OF THE RENEGADE*
2964—ANNIE AND THE RED HOT ITALIAN**

*The Scandalous St. Claires
**The Balfour Brides

Carole Mortimer

SURRENDER TO THE PAST

TORONTO NEW YORK LONDON
AMSTERDAM PARIS SYDNEY HAMBURG
STOCKHOLM ATHENS TOKYO MILAN MADRID
PRAGUE WARSAW BUDAPEST AUCKLAND

Recycling programs
for this product may
not exist in your area.

ISBN-13: 978-0-373-13043-6

SURRENDER TO THE PAST

First North American Publication 2012

Copyright © 2011 by Carole Mortimer

SURRENDER TO THE PAST

To Peter

CHAPTER ONE

'MIND if I join you?'

'Please do. I'm finished here, anyway.' The warmly polite words had already been spoken before Mia looked up, but the friendly smile curving her lips froze in place as she instantly recognised the man standing beside her booth in the crowded coffee shop.

How could she not recognise Ethan Black?

Big. Dark. Forceful. Arrogant. Magnetically attractive. Still...

Mia drew in a deep breath, chin tilting in challenge as she took in everything about him. It had been five years since she last saw Ethan, and his hair was still as dark as night, although it was styled much shorter than it used to be. Expertly so. His face was just as male-model handsome: wide, intelligent brow, penetrating grey eyes, sculptured cheekbones either side of a long straight nose, and a wickedly sinful mouth above a square and determined jaw. Although his mouth was unsmiling at the moment...

The same, and yet not the same.

Ethan would be thirty-one now, to Mia's twenty-five, and that maturity showed in the cynical depths of his eyes that at the moment had all the colour and warmth of a bleak winter sky. His cheeks were thinner too, more hollow, and there were lines beside his eyes and mouth that hadn't been there before either.

He was dressed in a black—obviously expensively tailored designer-label suit, with a black cashmere overcoat that reached mid-calf and drew attention to the handmade Italian shoes in soft black leather.

And he was nearly a foot taller than Mia's own five feet four inches—she was getting a crick in her neck just from looking up at him!

'Ethan.' She nodded tersely, knowing her initial reaction would have been too obvious for her to even attempt to act as if she hadn't recognised him.

Or realised that his presence at this particular coffee shop—the coffee shop Mia both owned and ran— couldn't simply be a coincidence...

There was, Mia realised warily, a hardness about Ethan as he looked down at her—an unsmiling, haughty demeanour totally in keeping with those other changes she had noted in his appearance. A powerful arrogance that so reminded Mia of the man Ethan worked for. Mia's father...

She raised her brows. 'You're supposed to buy the coffee and a cookie from the counter before you sit down.'

He shrugged, unconcerned. 'And if I don't want coffee or a cookie?'

Mia smiled ruefully. 'Then you obviously made a mistake coming into an establishment called Coffee and Cookies!'

'There was no mistake, Mia.'

'Of course not,' she accepted smoothly. 'The omnipotent Ethan Black doesn't make mistakes.'

Ethan eyed her coldly as he ignored the jibe. 'Do you think we could go somewhere more...private and talk?' He looked pointedly around the room, crowded with people laughing and chatting as they enjoyed their hot drinks and biscuits in the warmth of the cosy coffee shop.

''Fraid not.' Mia's light answer was completely bereft of apology as she closed the magazine she had been flicking through before his arrival. 'My afternoon break is over and, as you can see, we're a little busy right now.'

He didn't move, effectively blocking her in the booth. 'And I'm sure that as the owner you can take a break whenever you want to.'

'Then obviously I don't want to.' Mia wasn't in the least surprised that Ethan knew she owned the coffee shop; if he knew where to find her at four-thirty on a Thursday afternoon, then he would also have made a point of knowing she owned the coffee shop in which she could be found!

Ethan shrugged. 'Then I'll just sit here and wait until you finish work for the day.'

'Not without buying coffee and a cookie, you won't.'

'Then I'll do that,' he retorted. 'Or alternatively we can meet up somewhere once you've closed up for the day?'

Once upon a time—in another life!—Mia would have been delighted at the idea of meeting up with Ethan. Any time. Any place.

Once upon a time...

It sounded like the beginning of a fairytale. Probably because that was what her infatuation with Ethan had always been—nothing more than a complete flight of fantasy on Mia's part!

She sighed. 'How did you find me, Ethan?'

He looked at her from between narrowed lids. 'When your father has failed to do so in five years of searching?' he taunted.

Her mouth thinned. 'If that's how long he's looked, yes.'

Ethan grimaced. 'We really should go somewhere more private to discuss this, Mia.'

'I said no.'

Irritation darkened his brow. 'We *are* going to talk, Mia.'

'Whether I like it or not?'

'Yes.'

That was what Mia had thought! 'Did my father send you?'

Ethan gave a hard smile. 'No one "sends" me anywhere, Mia.'

'Meaning you volunteered to come and talk to me, or that my father doesn't even know you're here?' She eyed him sceptically.

'Both.' He was obviously not comfortable with the latter.

Mia eyed him warily. 'If my father didn't send you, then what possible reason could you have for being here, Ethan?'

'I've already told you—because I want to talk to you,' he muttered tersely.

'And if I don't want to talk to you?'

'You appear to be doing so, whether you want to or not!'

Yes, she did. And Mia had no intention of continuing to do so. 'I'm busy, Ethan.' She stood up.

Ethan gave a glance around the café. It was designed to be as warm and cosy as someone's sitting room, with comfortable armchairs grouped around low tables, and prints on the walls interspersed with plants trailing down from hooks fixed in the ceiling. The people sitting at those tables ranged in age from a mother and her young child—the latter obviously enjoying a hot chocolate with her cookie—several students from the university close by, who appeared to be working while they drank their coffee, to half a dozen or so older ladies, obviously meeting up for a chat in the late afternoon. Business, he noted abstractedly, was obviously thriving.

He turned back to look at the unmoving, grim-faced woman standing in the booth beside him. Mia had been twenty when Ethan had last seen her, with a prettily glowing face dominated by laughing green eyes, a nicely rounded body, and long straight hair the colour of ripe corn.

That softness was gone now. Her face was all hollows and angles, her body slim and toned—a fact only emphasised by the close-fitting black blouse and skin-tight black jeans. Her hair—that long and gloriously golden mane that had reached almost to her waist, and which Ethan clearly remembered falling softly, tantalisingly, across his bare flesh—was gone too. Although, he allowed grudgingly, the shorter, wispily feathered style certainly complemented the stark beauty of her face and emphasised the deep emerald colour of her eyes.

He gave a disbelieving shake of his head at the changes he saw in her. 'What happened to you, Mia?'

Her eyes narrowed. 'In what way?'

'In every way!' He scowled darkly. 'You're so changed in appearance that—'

'My own father wouldn't recognise me...?' she finished dryly.

Ethan stilled. 'I gather that was the point of the exercise?'

'Of course.'

Ethan's gaze raked over her critically. 'William might not recognise you, but I do. With or without your clothes!' he added.

Mia's breath left her in a loud hiss. 'That was uncalled-for!'

He gave a hard smile. 'I take it you didn't like my reference to the fact that we've been naked together?'

'I want you to leave, Ethan.' Her hands were clenched, her eyes glittering in warning. *'Now!'*

He looked down at her speculatively. 'I never would have imagined you even working in a coffee shop, let alone owning one...'

'And why is that?' Mia bristled. 'Did you imagine that the daughter of Kay Burton would be too frightened of breaking a nail if she actually worked?'

'I never once confused you with your mother, Mia,' he drawled softly.

Mia's mother...

A beautiful and accomplished hostess. A social butterfly. Until the accident nine years ago that had not only robbed Kay of her beauty but the use of her legs...

Mia's gaze fixed on Ethan. 'If you don't leave voluntarily in the next thirty seconds I'm going to call the police and have you forcibly removed!'

He looked at her in mock horror. 'On what grounds?'

'How about making a public nuisance of yourself? And I'm sure if I were to call the newspapers at least one of them would just love to come along and take pictures of Ethan Black being ejected from a coffee shop,' she taunted.

His mouth tightened and his eyes drew into icy slits of grey. 'Are you threatening me?'

'Does it sound as if I am?'

'Yes!'

'Then I probably am,' Mia confirmed.

'You do realise that even if I agree to leave now I'll only come back later?'

Oh, yes. Mia realised that… Having finally succeeded in finding her, she very much doubted that Ethan was now going to just walk away without saying exactly what he had come here to say…

It had been five years, for goodness' sake. Five years during which—as Ethan had just pointed out so cuttingly—Mia had changed almost beyond recognition. And those changes weren't just physical…

Five years ago she had been totally infatuated—in love with Ethan. An interest he had briefly—*very* briefly—seemed to reciprocate. That mutual interest had come to an abrupt end when Mia's mother died suddenly and Mia became aware of the fragility upon which her world had been built. A world she had thought so bright with possibilities suddenly made bereft and uncertain…

'Please yourself,' she dismissed dryly.

'I usually do.'

'Why am I not surprised?' Mia gave his own changed appearance another scathing glance. 'Working for my father all these years has not only resulted in you looking and dressing like him, but also talking like he does too—as if you're God Almighty!'

Ethan snorted his impatience. 'Insult me all you wish, Mia, but let's leave your father out of it.'

'Fine with me. You have ten seconds of the thirty left, Ethan.' Her expression remained unrelenting.

His mouth thinned, and he looked as if he would like to add more before nodding abruptly. 'As I said, I'll be back.' It was more of a warning than a promise.

A warning Mia had no intention of heeding. 'Ob-

viously I'm not going to say it was good seeing you
again.'

'I remember a time when you couldn't wait to see me.'
His hard eyes swept over her with slow deliberation. 'All
of me…'

The colour rose in Mia's cheeks as she was reminded
of just how well she had once known this man. 'Just
leave, will you, Ethan?'

He gave a mocking inclination of his head. 'For the
moment.'

Mia watched in frustration as Ethan turned on one
leather-shod heel and walked confidently over to the
door, turning briefly so his glittering silver gaze met
Mia's across the room once more in challenge, before
he stepped outside and closed the door quietly behind
him.

At which point all of Mia's outward bravado left her
like the air from a deflating balloon and she began to
hyperventilate. She had to rest her hands supportively
on the table-top as her knees began to shake…

'Are you feeling all right, Mia?' Dee, the nineteen-
year-old Mia employed to help out with the serving, gave
her a concerned glance as she cleared the neighbouring
booth.

Was Mia feeling all right? *No*, came back the de-
finitive answer. The last thing Mia was feeling was *all
right*!

It had been five long years, damn it! And Ethan had
just walked back into her life as if he had never left it.
Worse—that last threat confirmed that he had no intention of leaving it again until he had said what he wanted
to say to her.

'I think I need to go outside for some air.' She gave

Dee a wobbly smile. 'Can you and Matt manage here for a while longer?'

'No problem,' Dee assured her readily.

Mia stood up to move quickly through the coffee shop and out to the kitchen, grabbing up her short leather jacket and hurrying out through the back door to breathe in large gulps of the fresh September air before moving away from the coffee shop as if rabid dogs were at her heels. Or Ethan Black…

Ethan.

The man Mia had fantasised about for years until he had finally asked her out and every one of those fantasies had become reality.

The man she had once believed herself to be deeply in love with.

The same man Mia had just discovered was still capable of making her aware of every disturbing thing about him just by being in the same room with her!

CHAPTER TWO

'I THOUGHT you were in a hurry to get back to work?'

Mia hadn't even realised she was being followed as she hurried into the park at the end of the street, but she now came to an abrupt halt on the gravel pathway, eyes closing tightly, shoulders stiff, her jaw clenched, hands fisted at her sides, as Ethan spoke softly from just behind her.

All those years of silence. Of peace. And now she was being hounded by one of the very people she had so desperately needed to get away from. To the extent that Mia knew she would never be able to come to this park again without recalling Ethan's presence here, too.

'Mia...?'

She drew in a deeply controlling breath, smoothing her expression into one of mild uninterest before slowly turning to face Ethan.

'I could add harassment to that list of charges.' She eyed him defiantly.

To Ethan she had looked so very different inside the coffee shop. Not only looked different but acted differently too—like a distant stranger. But he could see traces of the old Mia in her now—in the depths of her eyes, the soft curve of her mouth, and the vulnerable tilt of her chin.

'I'm sure the police would have no interest in a stepbrother visiting his long-lost stepsister.' Ethan knew before he had finished speaking that it had been the wrong thing to say. Her eyes chilled over with obvious distaste at that connection between the two of them.

'You aren't my stepbrother, Ethan, because I disowned what was left of my family *before* your mother married my father four and a half years ago! And I wasn't lost—I just didn't want to be found. I still don't,' she added flatly.

'Too late!'

'Obviously.' She continued to eye him coldly.

Ethan knew that it was going to be up to him to stop baiting her in this way if this wasn't to develop into nothing more than a slanging match. Mia's resentment about the past was still such that it wasn't just going to evaporate during the course of one conversation. One conversation badly handled on his part, he acknowledged heavily.

He had been thrown slightly off-balance earlier, when he'd walked into the coffee shop and recognised Mia sitting in a booth at the back of the room reading a magazine. A Mia so changed, but at the same time so confident in the world she had created for herself, that for one heart-stopping moment Ethan had almost hesitated about disturbing her obvious contentment. Almost...

He gave a grimace. 'Could we start again, do you think...?'

'Where would you like to start from?' Her eyes glittered like emeralds in the pallor of her face. 'Perhaps when I first became a sixth-form pupil at the boarding school of which your widowed mother was headmistress? Or after your mother's affair with my father, perhaps? Or when you conveniently got a job working for

Burton Industries—my *father's* firm—once you'd left LSE with your first-class master's degree and a PhD? With hindsight you *have* to have realised the significance of that…?'

'The possibility I was only employed at Burton Industries because of my mother's…connection to your father?' Ethan drawled dryly. 'It crossed my mind, of course—'

'I'm sure it did!'

'And was as quickly dismissed,' he bit out harshly. 'I'm going to say this only once more, Mia—my mother *wasn't* involved with your father before you went to Southlands School. Nor did their later friendship have anything to do with my getting a job at Burton Industries.'

She smiled humourlessly. 'And "once more" I'm going to choose not to believe you!'

'Why am I not surprised?'

'Perhaps because to you at least I was always so predictable!'

He gave an impatient sigh. 'I was head-hunted by dozens of companies when I left university, Mia. Burton Industries were lucky to have me.'

They probably were, Mia conceded grudgingly; Ethan's qualifications had never been in question. Or his ambition. It was only the lengths he was willing to go to in order to achieve those ambitions that had become so glaringly questionable. Lengths which involved the once innocent and naively trusting Mia.

She had wondered five years ago—at the same time as she'd thanked her good fortune!—how she had ever been lucky enough to attract the attention of someone like Ethan Black. The epitome of tall, dark and handsome, he could—and usually did—have any woman that he wanted. Mia may have been the only daughter of multi-millionaire William Burton and beautiful socialite Kay, but beneath the fashionable designer-label clothes her mother had insisted on buying for her Mia had also been terribly shy, and merely pretty rather than beautiful, like the women Ethan was usually attracted to.

Once she'd learned of Ethan's mother's affair with her father, the reason for Ethan's attraction had become obvious: Grace had made a play for the father, Ethan the daughter. One of them was sure to succeed.

'And let's call our parents' past relationship the nasty little affair that it really was, shall we?' Mia's top lip turned back with distaste.

'I told you it wasn't like that—'

'I'm really not interested, Ethan.'

'No—because you prefer to twist events to suit your own warped take on what really happened five years ago.'

'Nothing of what I eventually learnt about that situation suited me, Ethan,' Mia assured him furiously. 'Certainly not the realization that the only reason my father had chosen that particular boarding school to send me to in the first place was so that he had an excuse to visit his mistress. That's quite a play on words, don't you think? My headmistress was also my father's mistress—'

'Stop it, Mia!' Ethan reached out to grasp the tops of her arms and shake her. 'Just stop it!'

'Let go of me, Ethan,' Mia gasped. 'You're hurting me!'

His fingers tightened rather than relaxed, her leather jacket proving no barrier to the pain of his fingers biting into her arms.

'I'm hurting you?' He thrust her firmly away from

him, his gaze raking over her mercilessly. 'Do you have any idea—any idea at all—of the heartache you caused your father—have continued to cause him—by just disappearing in that way five years ago?'

'But I'm sure my leaving didn't affect you in the same way—did it, Ethan?' she murmured scornfully.

'Would you believe me if I were to say yes?'

'No.'

His mouth tightened.

'God, I was such an innocent. Such a fool!' She gave a pained groan.

'Because you were attracted to me?'

'Because I was stupid enough to think that you were attracted to *me*!'

He frowned darkly. 'I *was* attracted to you—'

'Oh, please, Ethan.' Mia gave a fierce shake of her head. 'What you were attracted to was my father's bank account and Burton Industries. You and your mother, both!'

'I should be careful what you say next, Mia…' Ethan's tone was icy with warning.

A warning Mia had absolutely no interest in. 'At least I had the good sense to get out. Whereas my father—'

'I said *stop*, Mia.'

'It's really not important now anyway.' She gave an uninterested

shrug. 'Five years later you both appear to be exactly where you always wanted to be—your mother is married to my father and you're running Burton Industries!'

Ethan's face looked as if it had been carved out of stone. 'You really do believe that's all I wanted all along?'

'Oh, yes,' Mia assured him with feeling. 'You've always done exactly what was in the best interests of

Ethan Black! And—to set the record straight—I didn't *disappear* five years ago. I left.'

'You disappeared, damn it!' Ethan grimaced. 'Just dropped out part-way through your second year of university, dropped *me*, and left!'

'I was twenty years old. And, unless I'm mistaken, in this country that's classed as being an adult, capable of making your own decisions. Besides, I left my father a note—'

'"Don't bother looking for me because you won't find me."' Ethan quoted disgustedly. 'What the hell sort of letter is that to leave anyone—least of all the man who had loved and cared for you since the day you were born?'

Mia's eyes narrowed. 'Even that was more than he deserved!'

'More than he deserved...?' he repeated softly.

'Yes!' She didn't at all care for the revulsion she could read in Ethan's expression. 'And I only left him that much so he wouldn't decide to report me as missing to the police!'

'And what about me, Mia? What did I deserve? The two of us were dating, sleeping together, when you decided to pull that disappearing act!'

'It was the boss's daughter you were sleeping with, Ethan. Not me,' she dismissed scathingly.

'That isn't true.' Ethan frowned.

'Whether it's true or not is unimportant—now as well as then. Just knowing of your connection to the woman who helped to make a fool of my mother was—and still is—enough reason for me never to want to see or hear from you ever again,' Mia stated flatly.

Ethan drew in a ragged breath. 'Okay, let's forget about our own relationship if it makes you happy—'

'Oh, it does!'

'But William is your father—'

'Something—along with you and your mother—I've been trying to forget for the past five years!' She turned her back on him to walk away, and sat down on a wooden bench looking out over the parkland. She was hoping that Ethan wouldn't follow her, but was not altogether surprised when, after a few seconds' hesitation, he walked that same short distance and sat on the other end of the bench.

The two of them sat in uneasy silence for several long minutes.

'He didn't report you missing but he—we certainly looked for you.' Ethan finally broke that silence, his voice huskily soft.

'Don't bother with the "we", Ethan,' she cut in dryly. 'My father may have been too lovestruck by your mother to have realised it, but I certainly know that it wasn't in *your* best interests for me to be found.'

'Another piece of your own unique logic?'

'Not at all,' she said. 'Once I had been removed from the equation it allowed both you and your mother to move in on my father.'

'Damn you—'

'No doubt,' Mia accepted ruefully.

'Okay, I can see there's no reasoning with you on the subject of my mother or me—but what about your father?'

'What about him?'

'How could you just turn your back on him in that way?' Ethan gave an impatient shake of his head. 'William searched for you for months. Years! No lead was too small for him to follow up. No possible sighting of you too ridiculous for him to investigate.'

Mia didn't so much as glance at him. 'And to think that I never left London.'

'You—?' Ethan gave a disbelieving shake of his head. 'You were here in the city all the time?'

'Yes.' She gave a humourless smile. 'Don't look so shocked,

Ethan; haven't you heard that the best way to avoid detection by the enemy is by staying right under his nose!'

'None of us were ever your enemy.'

'No?'

'No!' Ethan eyed her in frustration. 'Damn it!' He began to pace. 'So where exactly *were* you in London?'

Mia's cheeks warmed at his obvious disgust. 'I stayed with friends for the first couple of months.'

'We—William contacted all of your friends to see if any of them had seen or heard from you and they all said they hadn't!'

She raised her brows. 'They were *my* friends, Ethan, not his.'

'With friends like that…!' His jaw tightened. 'Where did you go after you left these so-called friends?'

'I bought an apartment, took some classes, and then a couple of years ago I opened the coffee shop.'

'What sort of classes? William checked every year with all the universities to see if you were attending any of them,' he added with a frown.

'I enrolled in a very reputable cookery school right here in London, Ethan,' Mia announced with satisfaction.

'Cookery school…? You actually *bake* the cookies in Coffee and Cookies yourself?'

She almost laughed at the disbelief in Ethan's

expression. Almost. But even knowing she had managed to totally bemuse the arrogant Ethan Black wasn't enough reason for Mia to feel like laughing today. Nor was it reason enough to tell him that she not only baked cookies for her coffee shop but also for a couple of very upmarket specialist food stores in London…

'My maternal grandmother, as well as leaving me the hefty trust fund that my father so conveniently signed over to me on my eighteenth birthday, also taught me to bake. I'm good at it,' she added defensively as Ethan just continued to stare at her.

'I'm sure that you are.' Ethan finally nodded slowly. 'But it's a drastic change from the economics you were studying before you dropped out.'

She grimaced. 'That was always my father's choice, not mine.'

'Because he expected you to take over Burton Industries one day?'

'Probably,' Mia acknowledged. 'How lucky for him that you came along so conveniently to fill the breach.'

Ethan drew in a hissing breath. 'Bitter and twisted doesn't suit you, Mia.'

Her eyes flashed a deep dark green. 'This is me being a realist, Ethan, not bitter and twisted.'

'You closed your bank account two days after you left. We all thought you must have gone abroad somewhere.'

Mia gave another shrug. 'Because that's what you were all supposed to believe.'

'That was unbelievably cruel, Mia.'

Her eyes glittered. 'You don't know the meaning of the word!'

'Oh, believe me, I'm learning fast,' Ethan assured her grimly.

Mia fell silent, not looking at Ethan but at the people in the park—some walking their dogs, others taking their children home from school. All such everyday occurrences, sights and people Mia saw every day whenever she came to the park to eat her lunch, and yet Ethan's presence here made this totally unlike a normal day for her...

She turned to look at him where he sat on the other end of the bench, her heart tightening in her chest at the bleakness of his expression as he stared straight back at her.

He was more attractive than he had ever been, Mia grudgingly admitted. Those outward signs of maturity gave him a dangerous edge and that aura of arrogant self-confidence only added to the impression of danger.

Her chin rose. 'I forgot to congratulate you earlier. On your promotion,' she explained at Ethan's questioning glance. 'It was announced in the newspapers several months ago that you were made CEO of Burton Industries.'

He looked at her through narrowed lids. 'And did you also see in the newspapers the circumstances under which I became CEO of the company?'

Mia turned away from that piercing silver gaze. 'Because my father had a heart attack.'

'You knew William had been ill?' Ethan stared at her incredulously.

'Yes,' she confirmed flatly.

'And yet you still didn't go to see him?' Ethan made no effort to hide his disgust now. Mia had known—all the time she had known about William's heart attack—and she hadn't even bothered to telephone her father, let alone go to see him...

Her sighed heavily. 'Obviously not.'

'What if he had died, Mia, and you never saw him again?'

Mia tried not to shudder at the thought. As much as her father had hurt her badly, she still questioned whether she had done the right thing. But Ethan didn't need to know that, so she shrugged. 'I have no intention of ever seeing him again.'

'And what if I were to tell you that it was another erroneous sighting of you that caused his heart attack?'

'It's been five years, Ethan—don't try and lay that guilt trip on me!'

'Five years or fifty—your father will never stop loving you. Never stop looking for you!'

Her expression remained unrelenting. 'I'm not, nor have I ever been—obviously!—answerable for anything my father may or may not choose to do.'

Ethan looked at her for several long, tense seconds before standing up abruptly. 'I'm wasting my time even trying to talk to you, aren't I?' It was more a flat statement than a question.

'I'm glad you've finally realised that.' Mia looked up at him unemotionally.

He gave a shake of his head. 'Obviously the changes in you aren't just on the surface, but go all the way to your selfish and bitter little heart!'

'How dare you...?' Mia gasped.

Ethan looked down at her as if he had never seen her before. 'You were so beautiful, so sweet and trusting—'

'Well, I certainly had *that* knocked out of me, didn't I?' She eyed him wearily.

'Are you referring to me or to your father now?'

'Both!'

'Forget about me—'

'Oh, let's!'

Ethan gave an impatient shake of his head. 'William did everything for you. Loved you. Damn it, he *adored* you—'

'And then he betrayed everything I believed about him by having an affair with your mother!' Mia finished heatedly as she stood up to face him. 'And just because the two of them finally married each other it doesn't make your mother any more my stepmother than it makes *you* my stepbrother! None of those things changes the fact that long before *my* mother died my father was involved in an affair with your own mother.'

'It wasn't like that. You make it sound so—'

'Sordid?' she suggested. 'Maybe that's because it *was* sordid. My mother was in a wheelchair for the last four years of her life, and all the time my father and your mother—'

'I've told you—it wasn't all the time.' His eyes glittered. 'They didn't even know each other until after you started attending Southlands School.'

Mia gave an inelegant snort. 'You really expect me to believe that?'

'I'm telling you how it was—'

'And beware anyone who dares to disbelieve the arrogant and powerful Ethan Black?' She eyed him mockingly.

'This isn't about me, Mia. And it isn't about you, either,' he added grimly, cutting her off as she was about to speak. 'Yes, your father and my mother made the mistake of falling in love with each other while your father was still married, but they didn't do anything about those feelings until after your mother died. I know you would rather believe otherwise, but—'

'My God, I can't believe you actually fell for any of

that sanctimonious rubbish they spouted after my mother died.' She looked at him with pity. 'That whole story of how the two of them fell in love but fought against their feelings! I always gave you credit for having more intelligence than to believe something so lame, Ethan.'

He eyed her derisively. 'From what I've observed of the emotion, intelligence has very little to do with falling in love.'

'The two of them were together on the day my mother killed herself, Ethan,' she continued fiercely. 'They were together at your mother's house while my mother sat at home and downed a bottle of sleeping pills with a bottle of wine!'

He winced. 'Your mother didn't even know about their friendship.'

'How can you possibly know that?' Mia scorned. 'She didn't so much as leave a note, so how can anyone know what my mother was thinking when she swallowed that bottle of pills?'

Ethan hesitated, thinking of the promise William had extracted from both himself and his mother never to tell Mia of the real circumstances behind her mother's death, or the letter Kay had left for him. It was a promise they had both kept for the past five years. But at what price…?

He bit back his frustration. 'I'm sorry your mother did what she did, but you have to believe that it had nothing to do with the friendship that existed between my mother and your father.'

'I don't have to believe anything, Ethan.' Her face had paled to a ghostly white.

Damn it, Ethan hadn't come here to hurt Mia. Just like William, Ethan had never wanted to do that. 'Mia, I know how you must have felt—still feel—'

'You don't know anything about me, Ethan!' Mia shook her head. 'Certainly not how I felt then. Or how I still and will always feel about the circumstances of my mother's death.'

'Maybe that's because you refused all my attempts to see you after she died?' Ethan reminded her harshly.

Of course Mia had refused to see Ethan again after her mother had died and her father's affair with Ethan's mother had made front-page headlines in every newspaper in the country. How could she have done anything else, behaved in any other way, when the knowledge of that affair had shown her all too clearly the unfolding of past events and the reasons for them? *All* of them. Including the reason for her own brief relationship with Ethan.

'We had nothing left to say to each other, Ethan. You were just using me. Just—' Mia broke off abruptly as she heard her the emotional break in her voice.

She would *not* do this! She didn't care what Ethan thought of her now, what he accused her of—or how hurtful she found those accusations—she would not allow herself to be put through this emotional wringer a second time.

The worst part of it was that she had loved her father so much—worshipped him, almost. She had liked Grace Black too, for the two years she'd been a pupil at her school. Until she'd later found out about the affair.

As for her feelings for Ethan…!

She had worshipped him from afar for years too—already been crazily in love with him when he'd asked her out for the first time. She would have done anything—been anything that he wanted her to be. And all the time—all the time his mother had been involved in a relationship with Mia's father.

She dropped down abruptly onto the bench, her face averted. 'You're right, Ethan. We're done here.'

Ethan looked at the sharpness of her profile: pale and hollow cheeks, haunted eyes, the slenderness of her body poised as if for a fight.

He knew how much the past had hurt Mia. How much his own connection with the woman her father loved had and still did hurt her. But she would not believe—how could she, when she refused to believe everything else he told her?—how hurt and upset he had been about that friendship too, until William and his mother had explained the truth of the situation to him.

A truth that William had refused absolutely ever to confide in the grieving Mia, insisting that he had no intention of trying to win back his daughter's love at the cost of damaging Mia's memory of the mother she had loved.

Ethan thrust his clenched hands into the pockets of his overcoat. 'I take it you still know where the offices of Burton Industries are? If you should change your mind and decide you want to talk to me after all?'

'Yes.' She didn't even glance at him.

'But you aren't going to, are you…?'

Her mouth tightened. 'No.'

Ethan clearly remembered the first time he had seen Mia. He had been twenty-two, about to start his PhD at LSE, and Mia had been sixteen years old—a new sixth-form pupil at the school where his mother was headmistress. Her father had decided that it would be better for Mia to attend a boarding school after her mother had been involved in a car accident the year before, resulting in Kay being in a wheelchair, with her face badly scarred, and quite unable to deal with the needs of her young daughter.

It had been Mia's first time away from home, and she had obviously been very nervous at having tea, along with all the other new girls, at the home of her new headmistress.

She had stood silent and alone at the back of his mother's private sitting room, nothing at all like those other self-confident sixteen-year-old girls vying for the attention of the headmistress's son. Instead she had exuded all the vulnerability of a puppy taken too early from its mother: her eyes too big for her face, the corn-gold hair long and silky, a vulnerable curve to the delicacy of her chin.

Ethan had felt sorry for her—had realized that she couldn't know any of the other new girls yet. Her sweet shyness had revealed how traumatised she was at leaving her parents and her home for the first time, and it had seemed the most natural thing in the world for Ethan to go and talk to her, to ease some of her nervousness, and for a friendship of sorts to develop between the two of them after that initial meeting.

An intermittent friendship, admittedly, with Ethan away at university most of the time, but he had always made a point of seeing and speaking with Mia at least once when he came home for the weekend or holidays.

It had seemed entirely natural too that Ethan should take the job offered to him with her father's company when he finally left university, and it hadn't been that big a step when he'd seen Mia again, looking stunningly beautiful and completely grown up in a figure-hugging red gown as she acted as her father's hostess at the company Christmas party, for him to realise he was deeply attracted to this more mature Mia.

It had been an attraction she had seemed to more than reciprocate when she'd accepted his invitation to dinner, and the two of them had begun to see each other on a regular basis.

Ethan had dated often during his university years, and gone to bed with quite a few of those women, but his relationship with Mia hadn't been like anything he had known in the past: emotionally intense, and physically satisfying in a way Ethan had never experienced with anyone else. Then or since...

The woman now sitting on the park bench wasn't the Mia he had known. This woman wasn't in the least shy, and as for that appealing sweetness that had once brought out such a protective instinct in him—this older, assertive Mia was more like a Rottweiler than a defenceless puppy! So much so that Ethan certainly wouldn't have attempted to even take her in his arms, let alone make love with her.

Her expression was scornful now as she looked at him. 'Goodbye, Ethan.'

He sighed heavily. 'No matter what you may choose to believe to the contrary, Mia, my liking for you never had anything to do with my mother or my job at Burton Industries.'

Mia only heard the first part of that statement—Ethan had *'liked'* her! When Mia's naive and trusting heart had hoped that he would fall in love with her, as she had fallen in with him...

'How fortunate for you that you got over the emotion so quickly!'

Ethan gave a shake of his head. 'I don't know enough about who or what you are any more to know how I feel towards you now,' he acknowledged heavily. 'The Mia I once knew was sweet and warm, utterly enchanting, and I don't believe she would ever have deliberately hurt anyone, either.'

Her cheeks became flushed at the rebuke she heard in his tone. 'I had to grow up some time, Ethan.'

'So you did,' he accepted huskily.

And he obviously didn't like the way in which she *had* grown up! Well, that was just too bad—because Mia much preferred herself this way. Tougher. Stronger.

Ethan took a large brown envelope out of his pocket. 'You might like to have this.'

'What is it?' Mia said stiffly, totally ignoring the envelope he held out to her.

'Why don't you take a look inside and see?' He laid the envelope down on the bench beside her before turning and walking away.

Which was when the tears began to fall hotly, scaldingly down Mia's cheeks.

Damn!

Crying was the last thing Mia wanted to do. Instead she wanted to scream and shout, to wail against whatever cruel fate had brought Ethan back into her life.

Most of all she wanted to stop the aching agony that washed over her in increasingly painful waves just from seeing him again.

Instead, she picked up the brown envelope Ethan had left for her, ripping it open to tip the contents out onto the bench beside her.

And instantly felt all the colour drain from her cheeks...

CHAPTER THREE

'How dare you?' Mia stormed into Ethan's office on the top floor of the Burton Industries building the following morning, and threw the brown envelope down on top of the impressive oak desk in front of him, spilling the contents all over the papers he had obviously been signing when she'd burst unannounced into the room.

'I'm so sorry, Mr Black.' Ethan's flustered secretary had hurried into the room behind Mia. 'She just pushed her way in here before I had a chance to stop her—'

'It's okay, Trish,' Ethan assured her smoothly as he slowly placed his fountain pen down on the side of the desk. 'As this used to be the office of Miss Burton's father she obviously doesn't feel that she needs an appointment to see his successor.'

Mia heard the censure in Ethan's tone, and grudgingly admitted it was merited; after all, no matter what her personal opinion of her father might be, this was still his company.

'I apologise.' She turned to smile at Trish. 'I was just in such a hurry to see Ethan that I—well, I was obviously less than polite.'

'It was my fault entirely, Miss Burton.' The other woman looked even more embarrassed. 'I haven't been here very long, and I had no idea who—I'll make sure and show you straight in next time.' She smiled back tentatively.

As far as Mia was concerned there wouldn't be a next time; once she had told Ethan exactly what she thought of him she hoped never to have to see him again!

'Let's not go that far, Trish.' Ethan spoke dryly to his secretary, but that narrowed silver gaze was fixed steadily on Mia. 'I would like at least a little prior warning of the invasion!'

'I really am sorry, Mr Black. I honestly had no idea—'

'It's not a problem,' he assured her again smoothly. 'But thanks anyway. And could you call Jeff Bailey and tell him I may be a little late for the ten o'clock board meeting?'

'Certainly, Mr Black.' With a last apologetic smile in Mia's direction the other woman turned to leave.

'Just what do you think you were doing by—' Mia broke off in surprise as Ethan raised a silencing finger. A surprise she recovered from as soon as she heard his secretary closing the door on her way out. 'Don't you dare shush me, you arrogant, overbearing, pompous—'

'My, you're in good fighting form this morning, aren't you?' Ethan sat back in his high-backed black leather chair to consider her fully. Once again he was wearing one of those designer-label suits—charcoal-grey today—with a pale grey shirt and meticulously knotted tie. 'I had a feeling I might see you here some time this morning.'

'Then you weren't disappointed, were you?' Mia snapped. 'And you would have seen me last night if I had known where to find you.'

He nodded slowly. 'I moved apartments a couple of months ago.'

'No doubt you could afford to on a CEO's salary!'

His mouth tightened at the scorn in her voice. 'No doubt.'

Mia gave an impatient shake of her head. 'Explain exactly what you thought you were doing by having someone spying on me—taking photographs of me—' she lifted up the dozen coloured photographs that had fallen out of the brown envelope '—like some sort of pervert hiding in the bushes.'

'How else was I supposed to find you?'

'You weren't.' She stated the obvious.

He gave an unconcerned shrug. 'Too late.'

'You had no right spying on me, prying into my private life—'

'I don't consider locating the daughter of my stepfather to be prying into anything,' Ethan cut in coldly.

Mia became very still. His *stepfather*. Much as she might have tried to forget it the previous day, that did also made him her stepbrother. Oh, God...!

Ethan took advantage of Mia's momentary silence to take in her appearance. She was wearing a sweater in the same emerald-green as her eyes beneath a short black leather jacket, along with skin-tight low-rider denim jeans that left little to the imagination in regard to the taut roundness of her bottom and the slender length of her legs.

Not that Ethan needed to use his imagination where Mia was concerned; he knew exactly what she looked like naked. Or at least he had...

Mia was so much more slender than she'd used to be, but her skin—always the colour of ivory touched with a light rose, soft as velvet and begging to be touched—was just as appealing as it had always been. The fullness of her breasts would no longer be a snug fit in his hands, but the rounded curve of her bottom would, and he could imagine that softness as he pulled her into him and—

What the hell was he doing, fantasising about making love to Mia? Present tense, not past…

Damn it, wasn't this situation complicated enough already, due to the limited amount of information he felt able to share with Mia, without clouding the issue by resurrecting his desire for this woman that had once been so unrelenting? A desire Mia had made it more than obvious she would never feel for him again…

Ethan stood up restlessly. And instantly realised his mistake as the pulsing of his erection told him that it wasn't only his thoughts that had become wayward in the last few minutes!

He turned away to look out of the window rather than allowing Mia to see the evidence of his arousal. Yesterday he had been certain that he didn't even *like* this new tough and forceful Mia. Now his traitorous body had decided something completely different!

Not just his body, Ethan acknowledged with a frown. He had caught a glimpse of a softer, more appealing Mia just now, when she'd apologised to Trish for her rudeness, and that glimpse, it seemed, had been enough to reawaken the desire Ethan had felt for Mia since he had looked across the room where the company party was being held and seen her in that snug-fitting red dress, her hair a glorious gold tumble down the length of her spine…

'Who took those photographs, Ethan?'

Get a grip, Ethan, he instructed himself firmly. Stop thinking about taking Mia to bed and concentrate on the here and now. 'I hired a private security firm six months ago,' he revealed tautly.

'Obviously a more efficient one than my father.'

'Obviously,' Ethan said.

Mia had felt physically sick yesterday as she'd looked through the photographs inside the envelope Ethan had given her.

Photographs of her opening Coffee and Cookies in the morning. Of her walking alone in the park during her lunch break. Of her loading boxes of cookies into her car for delivery. Another one of her getting into her car and driving off. The list just went sickeningly on and on!

Someone—some unknown, faceless person Ethan had hired—had been following her, taking photographs of her, and she hadn't even realised it! 'Did my father ask you to do this?'

'No.'

'Then I don't understand...'

'Obviously not.' Ethan turned back to face her, eyes a glittering silver-grey. 'You already know your father had a heart attack six months ago, Mia,' he reminded grimly.

'Yes...'

'And the one thing he wanted before he died was to see you again.'

'How sweet!'

'Don't, Mia.' Ethan's warning was icily chill, his eyes becoming like silver shards of glittering glass.

'Don't what?' she taunted.

'Don't mock what you so obviously can't begin to understand.'

'Are you daring to question the love I felt for my father?'

'Obviously in the past tense,' Ethan recognised harshly. 'But, whether you like it or not, whether you accept it or not,' he added firmly, 'William will never stop loving you.'

'He has your mother now.'

'Considering what a cold-hearted little witch his daughter has turned into, that's probably as well!' He looked at her coldly.

Mia's cheeks flushed. 'You know nothing about me—'

'I know that you have only a few close female friends, that there's no current man in your life, and that you work twelve hours a day, six days a week in your coffee-shop.'

'Exactly how long did you have me watched, Ethan?' Mia's hands shook as she clenched them at her sides.

'It took almost the whole six months and a lot of man hours to find you.' He shrugged. 'The fact that you used only the name of a company to buy your coffee shop was what threw us off the scent for so long.' He looked at her reprovingly.

Mia's mouth firmed. 'And once you had found me?'

'A few days.'

'How many?'

'Five,' he stated flatly.

'I want any written reports on me given to you by this "private security firm".' Mia was breathing unevenly, not sure if she was just furious at having her private life invaded in this way, or if it was the fact that Ethan had instigated the search that made it seem so much more of an intrusion.

Ethan shrugged broad shoulders. 'I've already shred-ded them.'

Her eyes narrowed. 'Why?'

'Because they weren't relevant now that I've seen you

again,' Ethan dismissed impatiently, before moving to sit back behind his desk; he didn't need a written report on Mia to remember what was in it. To know there was no current male in Mia's life...

'It's relevant to *me*—'

'It's gone, Mia.' Ethan sighed. 'Destroyed. Unimportant.'

'Why should I believe you?'

His mouth tightened at her obvious scepticism. 'Perhaps because I have no reason to lie to you?'

'Did you ever need a reason?'

'Damn it, Mia—'

'Have you told my father yet that you've found and spoken to me?'

'Not yet, no,' Ethan bit out tersely.

'Why not...?' She eyed him guardedly.

He shrugged. 'I didn't feel able to do that without first speaking to you.'

'And now that you *have* spoken to me?'

Ethan breathed deeply. 'I see little point in telling him anything when you're obviously still so hostile to the idea of seeing him again.'

'That isn't going to change any time soon.' Inwardly, Mia told herself she had absolutely no intention of feeling in the least bit guilty over her refusal to see or hear from her father again.

'It might.'

'It won't,' she assured him evenly. 'Seeing you again—twice!—has been quite bad enough, thank you very much!'

'I can't see why. Unless I actually meant something to you five years ago...?'

'You didn't.' Mia gave a decisive shake of her head.

'You're just a part of something that I would rather forget.'

And that had been, and always would be, the problem between the two of them, Ethan acknowledged heavily. Even if they could have overcome the hurdle of the mistrust Mia felt in regard to him, Ethan still knew that every time Mia so much as looked at him now she was reminded of her mother's suicide five years ago. Along with the remorseless publicity that had followed because of her father's relationship with Ethan's mother.

What would Mia say or do if Ethan were to act on the desire that now raged through his body at the very thought of having all her restless aggression in his bed?

'Ethan!' Mia was obviously as irritated with his distraction as Ethan was.

He frowned his impatience. 'You've become quite the little spitfire, haven't you?'

'And?'

'I like it.' He shrugged.

She seemed dumbstruck for a few seconds, and then she glared at him. 'I have absolutely no interest in hearing what your opinion is of me now, Ethan!'

'Are you sure about that?'

Could Ethan possibly be flirting with her? Mia questioned incredulously. After all that had happened, their chequered history, was he actually—? No, he couldn't be. Ethan had made it perfectly clear that—spitfire apart— he didn't even *like* the woman she was now. That he thought she was both cruel and selfish.

When Mia was neither of those things...

Walking away from her father—from Ethan—from the only life and home she had ever known—had been the hardest thing Mia had ever had to do. But to have stayed when she'd felt as if everyone she had ever loved and cared for was either gone or had betrayed her— her mother by dying, her father and Ethan by deceiving her—would have been even harder.

And if Ethan thought it had been easy for her to stay away after she had read about her father's heart attack in the newspapers, then he was mistaken; if anything that had been more difficult to do than walking away initially.

Instead she had continued to follow her father's medical progress in those newspapers, to inwardly ache at the changes she saw in him when he was photographed leaving hospital two weeks after his heart attack. Her father's hair was iron-grey now, and there were lines on his face that certainly hadn't been there four and a half years ago. She had been pleased to see he looked slightly less strained and ill when he'd been photographed again four weeks later, boarding a plane on his way to recuperate at his home in the South of France. Although that pleasure had been somewhat diluted by seeing a smiling Grace Burton at his side...

'Could we get back to the reason I came here?' she prompted testily.

'Which was?'

'To tell you to call off your private security company, for one!' She began to pace restlessly.

'Already done. Anything else?'

'I want you out of my life. And I want you to stay out!' Her eyes flashed in warning.

'You seriously think, after all these months of searching, I'm now going to just give up on you because you tell me to?' Ethan raised his brows in derision.

'Why not? I gave up on all of you years ago!'

Ethan was well aware of that fact. But there were still

so many things that Mia didn't know about the past. Things that William had made Grace and Ethan promise never to tell her...

Such as the fact that Kay Burton had been about to leave both her daughter and her husband for a younger man—her tennis coach; how clichéd was that?—on the day of the car accident that had left her so badly injured and then in hospital for months afterwards. Such as the fact that the man Kay had been leaving her family for had decided he was no longer interested in being with a woman—even one as wealthy as Kay Burton would be after her divorce—who was badly scarred and would be confined to a wheelchair for the rest of her life. That had resulted in William feeling duty-bound to stand by the mother of his heartbroken daughter, even though she had been leaving him for another man and there had no longer been any love between himself and Kay.

The tennis coach hadn't completely disappeared from their lives, either...

The wealthy divorcee Kay no longer being an option, as far as the other man was concerned, he had instead decided to blackmail William in order to keep the truth of her mother's affair, of Kay's intention to leave her husband and daughter, from the already traumatised sixteen-year-old Mia. Blackmail that had only come to an end when Kay had killed herself and Mia had disappeared only days after her mother's funeral.

Not a pretty story, by any means—and certainly not one that William would have confided in his young daughter while her mother was still alive. And he had adamantly refused to tell Mia after Kay Burton took her own life.

Putting Ethan in a very precarious position now he had found Mia again. His respect for William dictated that he couldn't break his promise to the other man and tell Mia the truth—but, having now found her again, spoken with her, Ethan couldn't just walk away again either.

Even if he wanted to. Which he didn't. And not just because of his love for William; this older, self-reliant and more self-confident Mia was even more intriguing than the younger, vulnerable Mia had been...

He straightened determinedly. 'I'm not going anywhere, Mia.'

'Pity!'

'Isn't it?' he came back insincerely. 'So, why isn't there currently a man in your life, Mia?'

Mia was thrown slightly off-balance by this sudden change of subject. 'Is there currently a woman in your own life?' she counter-challenged.

'No,' he answered.

Her brows rose. 'Why not?'

Ethan gave a rueful shrug. 'Perhaps I'm a little more... discerning about the women who share my bed than I used to be?'

'You—'

'Arrogant? Overbearing? Pompous?'

'Absolute pig!' Mia completed forcefully.

'Sticks and stones, Mia,' Ethan dismissed derisively.

Mia stared across at him for several long seconds. Ethan was so different from the man she remembered from that first meeting nine years ago, and from when they had dated each other—slept together!—four years later. Both in looks and temperament.

She would never verbally admit to it, but she found this more mature Ethan slightly intimidating. Ruggedly handsome enough to set any woman's pulse racing, with a cool arrogance that attracted as much as it challenged. Quite a heady combination, in fact...

And Mia would be insane to ever allow herself to become attracted to Ethan all over again!

Her chin rose defiantly. 'I'm not joking here, Ethan; I want you out of my life.'

The previous teasing left his face. 'Disappear like you did, you mean?'

'As long as you stay out of my life I don't care what you choose to call it.'

He gave a slow shake of his head. 'We both know I can't do that.'

'Of course you can,' she reasoned impatiently. 'You just shred those photographs, like you did the written file, and forget you ever saw me.'

Ethan eyed her impatiently. 'You really think I can do that?'

'It's exactly what I intend doing where you're concerned.'

His mouth thinned. 'And what happens if William should have another heart attack? Do I still "forget" that I know exactly where you are? That I ever saw you again?'

Mia gave a pained frown. 'There's no reason to think my father will have another heart attack. Is there...?' she added uncertainly.

'There's no reason to think he won't, either,' Ethan rasped impatiently.

She gave an exasperated shake of her head. 'I'm leaving now, Ethan, and I don't ever want to see you again.'

'Want all you like, Mia; it isn't going to happen,' he came back mildly.

She gave him one last frustrated glare before turning on her heel and leaving, knowing Ethan well enough to realise he meant exactly what he said.

CHAPTER FOUR

'I THOUGHT I had made my feelings more than clear earlier today about seeing you again, Ethan?' Mia eyed him
impatiently as he stood by the counter, arms crossed in
front of his powerful chest, having arrived at Coffee and
Cookies a few minutes before closing time, but making
no effort to leave when the other customers did so.

'You did, yes,' he confirmed.

'But you, being you, decided to ignore me?'

'As I told you I would, yes.' He nodded unapologetically.

Mia wished that Ethan didn't look so heart-stoppingly
handsome this evening, having taken off his jacket and
draped it over one of the chairs to reveal a tight-fit-
ting black polo shirt beneath that defined his muscled
chest and arms, and a pair of well-worn denims that
fitted snugly in all the right—wrong?—places. He was
looking much more like the devastatingly handsome
Ethan she had once known so intimately—and loved so
completely!

Mia delayed answering by turning away to pull down
the blind on the front window, at the same time willing her pulse to stop racing and her cheeks to cease
burning.

She might have been completely thrown when Ethan

turned up at Coffee and Cookies but the impressionable Dee had been delighted; obviously Ethan was just as devastating to the female population as he had always been!

But not to her, Mia told herself firmly. She was well and truly over Ethan Black. Had been over him for years.

And wasn't she protesting just a little too much…?

Not when it came to Ethan, no! He had always been a force to be reckoned with, but the last five years had added a hard edge only a fool would deliberately choose to ignore. And Mia was no longer a fool.

'I thought the two of us could go out to dinner.'

Mia turned sharply. 'What?'

'Dinner. You and me. Together.'

Her cheeks felt warm. 'I'm just not getting through to you at all, am I? Let me repeat—I didn't want to see you again, let alone go out to dinner or anything else with you.'

'Perhaps you should wait until you're asked for anything else before turning it down?' he came back tauntingly.

Her eyed narrowed. 'You're really starting to irritate me now, Ethan.'

'Only starting?' He raised dark brows as he stood, effectively blocking her way, as she tried to move around him to the counter.

Mia breathed her impatience as Ethan stood tall and impenetrable in front of her. 'Isn't there someone else you could go and annoy this evening?'

'No doubt many, many people.' He nodded slowly, grey eyes looking down at her.

Mia wasn't sure she could cope with Ethan in this lighter mood. It reminded her far too forcibly and uncomfortably of how it had once been between them. In another lifetime. Between two other people...

'But I'm having far too much fun irritating *you* at the moment to want to be anywhere else,' he assured her dryly.

She looked up at him. 'Were you always this annoying, or is it something new?'

He gave an unconcerned shrug. 'Considering we virtually lived together for three months, you would no doubt be a better judge of that than me.'

No doubt...

Just thinking of that three months when she and Ethan had been together constantly, night as well as day, was enough to cause an ache in Mia's chest.

God, how she had loved him! She hadn't been able to get enough of his company. Or their lovemaking...

Long, pleasurable hours of just touching, caressing, kissing each other, before coming together in slow and pleasurable strokes until they both reached a climax that left them trembling in each other's arms. Or those other times, when they had been so hungry for each other they had barely been able to rid themselves of their clothes before falling on each other ravenously, their coupling wild, their orgasms earth-shattering.

Yes, she had loved Ethan—been in love with him, Mia acknowledged inwardly, but Ethan's emotions had been nowhere near as engaged. He had been twenty-six years old, very ambitious, and Mia had been a sweet and tasty morsel for him to seduce and devour on his single-minded way to the top. He certainly hadn't been in love with Mia as she had with him.

But Mia had not found a single thing about him annoying or irritating...

She gave a weary shake of her head. 'It's been a long day, and I'm too tired to eat, Ethan.'

He eyed the half a dozen cookies she had left over from today's sales. 'Can I try one?'

'Go ahead.' She nodded uninterestedly.

He examined the four different flavours on the plate. 'Which would you recommend?'

'The triple chocolate is always popular.'

'Great. You know—' He ceased talking as he took a bite of the cookie. 'Mmm. Wow! This is…' He took another bite. 'My God, this is—' He stopped talking again, eyes closed as he continued to munch on the cookie.

Mia gave Ethan a rueful glance—and then wished she hadn't as the expression on his face vividly reminded her of the way he had looked when they had made love together: eyes closed, a slight flush to those hard cheeks, lips so soft and seductive—

His eyes opened in surprise. 'This is *delicious.* Sinfully so,' he added huskily, his eyes a dark and velvet grey. 'You weren't joking when you said you were good at this.' He polished off the last of the cookie.

'Thank you. That will be a pound,' she added briskly.

'For one cookie?'

'Haven't you learnt yet, Ethan, that nothing in life is free?'

'True.' He placed a pound coin on the counter. 'Just so that you know I always pay my debts… You *are* looking a little tired,' he murmured as he gave her a considering glance. 'We can stay in and eat if you would prefer it? I'll cook,' he added dismissively as the derisive raising of Mia's brows told him she wasn't about to offer to cook for him.

'You cook now?'

It had always been something of a joke between the two of them in the past that Ethan didn't cook. Not couldn't—*didn't*. Living at the school with his mother meant that he had never had to bother preparing his own meals, and his culinary skills at university had consisted of ready-prepared meals and take-outs.

Ethan raised challenging brows. 'Try me.'

Once again Mia's heart gave an involuntary leap in her chest. Quickly followed by her imagination running riot as she considered in what way she might like to 'try' Ethan!

Which was utterly ridiculous. She hadn't meant anything to Ethan five years ago, and she didn't mean anything to him now except as her father's runaway daughter. Just as Ethan now meant absolutely nothing to her!

'Come on, Mia, it will be just like old times...'

He shouldn't—couldn't—be allowed to just walk back into her life as if the last five years had never been. As if the pain of once loving him to distraction had never existed.

Mia's shoulders straightened with her renewed resolve. 'I'm going out with friends this evening.'

Ethan's mouth thinned. 'The same friends who lied to your father five years ago and caused him so much added grief?'

She drew her breath in sharply at the rebuke. 'At least they were there for me, Ethan.'

'I would have been there for you too, if you had let me,' he said softly.

'Really? In what way would *you* have been there for me, Ethan?' she scoffed with a slow shake of her head. 'I may have been naively trusting five years ago, but I assure you that's no longer the case.'

Ethan eyed her with pent-up frustration. He had

always known that finding Mia again and talking to her would only be half the battle. Getting her to trust him again—enough to persuade her into seeing her father—was going to be so much harder to do...

He gave a rueful grimace. 'You weren't naive, Mia, you were beautiful, and totally without affectation.'

'Naive,' she repeated firmly. 'But luckily for me I grew up. Certainly enough to have more sense than to ever be attracted to someone like you again!'

Ethan raised dark brows. 'Is that the truth, or an invitation for me to prove you wrong...?'

Her eyes widened. In anger or alarm? Ethan hadn't learnt to read this more sophisticated and self-confident Mia yet.

'You'll know when—or if—I ever issue such an invitation, Ethan!' She glared her indignation.

Anger, Ethan acknowledged self-derisively. Which was a pity, because he had a feeling he would have very much enjoyed attempting to prove Mia wrong...

'Okay,' he accepted briskly. 'So where are we going?' He picked his jacket up from the back of the chair he had draped it over earlier.

'We aren't going anywhere,' Mia answered firmly. 'You're leaving to go...wherever, and I'm going out to meet up with friends. Alone.'

Ethan folded his arms in front of his chest. 'I don't think so, Mia.'

A frown appeared between Mia's clear green eyes. 'What do you mean...?'

He shrugged broad shoulders. 'I mean that now I've found you again I have no intention of your doing another disappearing act as soon as my back is turned.'

'As you are well aware, I now have a business to run—

which means I'm not free to just up and go anywhere any more.'

He gave a confident smile. 'Which is how I know exactly where you will be, Tuesday to Friday from ten o'clock in the morning until seven o'clock at night, and ten o'clock until five on Saturdays.'

Mia gave him a scathing glance. 'No doubt that was in the report supplied by your private security company!'

'No doubt.'

'What else did it tell you about me, Ethan?' Her voice was deceptively soft; Mia absolutely hated the fact that Ethan had not only found her but had actually had her investigated as well as photographed.

He gave another shrug. 'We've already covered the personal stuff,' he dismissed. 'Business-wise you're in profit, and have been for some time. You don't rent or lease this building, but bought it outright three years ago—obviously from the trust fund left to you by your maternal grandmother. You also supply boxes of Mia's Cookies on a regular basis to a number of reputable speciality shops in the city.'

'That's enough,' Mia instructed shakily as Ethan casually broke her life down to a series of unemotional statements. 'Not having been given a similar file on you, I'm obviously at something of a disadvantage.' She met his gaze challengingly.

Ethan relaxed back against the counter. 'What do you want to know?'

'Everything there is to know,' she said firmly.

Much as Mia might wish to deny it—to wish it wasn't true—on a physical level she was very aware of Ethan. Of the slight dampness to his hair from the shower he had probably taken before coming here. Of the way he smelt of soap and an elusively spicy aftershave. Of the way his eyes crinkled at the corners when he smiled, and how they became like shards of pale grey ice when he was angry or displeased. Of how the broad width of his shoulders and washboard flatness of his muscled chest and abdomen were clearly revealed in the black polo shirt, the muscles in his arms bulging as he continued to cross them in front of his chest. Of the way the snug fit of those jeans emphasised the leanness of his hips and the long length of his legs...

Mia had dated several men over the last few years—nice, pleasant men who posed no threat whatsoever to the even tenor of her life, let alone her heart; Ethan Black had always posed a threat to both those things. Just looking at him now, being with him again, told her that he still did...

Ethan watched through narrowed lids as the emotions flickered across the beauty of her ivory and cream face: angry challenge, frustration, followed by uncertainty. It was that last emotion that intrigued him the most.

'Okay.' He straightened. 'In my case, we've covered the business stuff. And the fact that I've recently changed apartments. You already know that there's no particular woman in my life at the moment, but I do go out socially a couple of times a week. I also fly over to visit the parents in the South of France every other weekend—'

'That's enough, thank you, Ethan,' Mia cut in.

'Sure?' He raised mocking brows. 'I haven't got to the good stuff yet.'

'I said I've heard enough!' Her eyes glittered deeply green.

'Fine.' He straightened. 'Did we decide yet where we're going? Staying here to eat, going out to dinner, or off to visit your friends?'

Mia frowned her frustration with his persistence. 'You

really can't just walk in here and attempt to take over my life—'

'Oh, I really can, Mia,' Ethan assured her mildly. 'In fact, I believe I already have.'

'For how long this time?'

His jaw was set grimly. 'For as long as it takes for you to agree to see your father again.'

All conversations between the two of them led back to her father, Mia acknowledged heavily. Selfish, Ethan had called Mia's behaviour five years ago. And maybe it had been. But she had been hurting so badly after her mother's death and the media exposure of her father's relationship with Grace Black, and the fact that the knowledge had made a complete nonsense of her relationship with Ethan. Especially so when Mia had realised that, although she had so obviously been in love with him, Ethan had never once told her he felt that way about her...

If she were honest with herself, that wrench from Ethan had been just as hard as distancing herself from her father. But it had been a parting Mia had known was totally necessary for her own pride, let alone self-protection...

She gave a shake of her head. 'We'll both be old and grey by the time that happens!'

He gave an impatient shake of his head. 'Your father would be long dead himself if that were the case!'

If Ethan had meant to disconcert Mia by that statement then he'd succeeded! Her father would be aged in his late fifties now, and with one heart attack already behind him...

'Did it ever occur to you that a sudden reappearance by me might only result in his having another heart attack?'

'I would make sure he was pre-warned of your visit first, of course,' Ethan dismissed dryly.

'Of course,' Mia murmured. 'But I wouldn't hold your breath, if I were you!'

'Don't worry. I won't.'

'Oh, I'm not in the least worried.'

Ethan continued to look at her through narrowed eyes for several seconds, before shrugging off the irritation he obviously felt at her stubbornness. 'Do you think we could we just go out and get some dinner? The cookie really was good, but I'm actually hungry for some real food.'

Mia knew from the arrogantly inmovable expression on Ethan's face that she could go on refusing to have dinner with him and it ultimately wasn't going to make the slightest bit of difference. Ethan's resolve was every bit as strong as her own. And she certainly had no intention of inviting him upstairs to her apartment or taking him out with her friends!

'Okay, Ethan.' She sighed. 'You can buy me dinner. I'd prefer Chinese, but if you have some other preference...?'

'Chinese it is.' Ethan nodded as he shrugged into his black jacket. 'Hey, we could always go to The Peking Chicken—'

'No!' There was no way, absolutely no way, Mia intended going to a restaurant the two of them had often been to together five years ago! Even their pet name for the restaurant—The Peking Chicken, rather than its real name of The Peking Duck—was enough to evoke memories Mia would rather forget. 'I've found a much better one that's closer to the coffee shop. It's a fifteen-minute walk, or we could drive there...?'

'My car is parked outside.' If Ethan was disappointed

not to be going to The Peking Duck there was no indication of it in his uninterested expression.

Mia glanced out of the window at the sleek black
car parked next to the pavement directly outside the
coffee shop. She nodded. 'I'll just need to go upstairs
and change first.'

'Am I okay as I am, or do I need to change too?'

Mia had no choice but to acknowledge Ethan was
more than 'okay' as he was. Her gaze was once again
drawn—magnetised!—to that broad expanse of Ethan's
shoulders and chest. Dark hair was visible at the open
neck of his shirt. A light dusting of dark hair that she
knew formed a vee over his chest and down over the
flatness of his abdomen, before disappearing—

'No, you don't need to change,' she rasped harshly,
her gaze once more on the hard planes of his face. A
face so achingly familiar and yet at the same time not;
Mia didn't remember Ethan's eyes being so frosty, his
jawline so arrogantly confident, or that cynical curve to
those sculptured lips.

Ethan claimed she had changed this past five years,
but Mia only had to look at him to know that he had
changed too...

She turned towards the back of the coffee shop.

'Where do you think you're going?' Mia was frowning as she realised Ethan was following her as she
walked down the hallway to the stairs that led up to her
apartment.

He raised dark brows. 'You said you were going upstairs to change...'

'And?'

'And I'm going with you, of course.'

'There's no "of course" about it, Ethan.' Her frown
deepened just at the thought of Ethan being anywhere

near the sanctuary she considered her apartment to be. He had already invaded the satisfaction she felt in the success of the coffee shop, and the peace she had always found by walking in the park; allowing him to go upstairs and ruin the privacy of her apartment was definitely not on the agenda. 'I'll only be gone a couple of minutes. You can wait for me down here.'

Ethan studied her. That Mia didn't want him in her apartment was obvious. Because she didn't want him in her home? Or could she possibly be nervous at the thought of being alone with him in the privacy of her apartment, with a bedroom close by?

What the hell—?

Ethan had never thought of himself as a masochist, but he had to be even to think about Mia and a bedroom in the same sentence!

Mia had made it pretty obvious—when she'd left him five years ago without so much as a goodbye, and again in her attitude towards him this past couple of days— that she had absolutely no interest in resurrecting even their old friendship, let alone the intimacy that had once existed between them.

Any more than he did?

Ethan found this changed Mia intriguing, yes, but the distrust she felt towards him, and made no effort to hide rendered it a madness on his part even to think about becoming involved with Mia a second time.

Even if it seemed he had been able to think of little else but making love to Mia again since seeing her again yesterday?

Since *before* he had met her again yesterday, if Ethan were completely honest…

After months of intensive searching for Mia, Ethan had almost given up hope of the security company he had hired being any more successful than William's, and he couldn't have been more surprised when someone from that company had come to see him two days ago with the news they believed they had finally found her.

Nor had Ethan initially recognised the woman who appeared in the photographs they had brought to him for verification...

The self-confident beauty in the photographs bore little resemblance to the younger, slightly plumper Mia, and it had only been when Ethan looked into the woman's eyes that he'd finally become convinced it really was her after all; he had always loved the deep colour of Mia's eyes.

Although admittedly that had been five years ago, when they had glowed with the joy of simply being alive rather than being scornfully dismissive as they had been yesterday, or warily guarded as they were this evening.

Showing more clearly than anything else ever could have done how distrustful she was of both Ethan and his motives for being here.

Deservedly so, when Ethan thought of the real reason he was here this evening...

CHAPTER FIVE

'NICE,' Mia commented dryly as Ethan pressed the button to unlock his car, before moving to hold open the passenger door of the black sports car for her to climb inside. And it literally *was* a climb, making Mia feel relieved that she was wearing fitted black trousers. She had a feeling she would have shown Ethan a lot more than her legs when she slid into the passenger seat if she had been wearing a skirt!

Ethan closed the door and moved around the car to get in beside her before commenting, 'No cracks about my being able to afford to own a car like this on a CEO's wages?'

He had been this way when Mia had rejoined him downstairs—cool and distant, as if he regretted those few minutes of teasing conversation between them earlier. Which was just fine with Mia; she preferred to keep things between them cool and distant too!

'Not really,' she dismissed with a grimace as the powerful engine roared into life. 'I somehow thought you would be married by now, possibly with a brood of young kids. Think how much they would have enjoyed drooling and drawing over the upholstery of Daddy's expensive car!'

'Do you think you could try saying that with a little less relish?' Ethan drawled ruefully.

Especially when it wasn't relish she was feeling, Mia recognised self-disgustedly; just the idea of Ethan being married, let alone a father, was enough to cause a cold shiver to run down the length of her spine.

Which was utterly ridiculous! After all that had happened Mia could have absolutely no personal interest in Ethan, so why should it bother her if some faceless woman was stupid enough to marry him, let alone have his children?

Except that it did...

Agreeing to go out to dinner with Ethan—even if it had been under duress!—was a bad idea. A very bad idea. Spending any time in his company was a bad idea if it was going to produce thoughts like these!

'Why did you think I would be married?'

Mia turned to look at him, her eyes wide, even slightly panicked at the realisation that she hadn't just thought Ethan would be married by now—she had hoped he would be!

Mia's trauma at learning of her father's relationship with Grace Black had given her a total disgust for extramarital affairs, meaning that a married Ethan would have been completely out of bounds. Totally beyond Mia's reach, in fact. Instead of which...

She gave a shrug of uninterest she was far from feeling. 'A wife and the statistical two point four children would seem to be the next logical step after being Manager, MD and now CEO.'

'Really?'

'Why not?'

He grimaced. 'I happen to believe you should find the right woman before even thinking of marriage.'

'And you never found her...?'

His mouth thinned. 'Obviously not, as I'm still single.'

Reminding Mia that *she* had once longed to be the woman that Ethan married. Not only longed for it, but dreamt about it. She would sit for hours imagining their wedding day, the wonderful house they would live in, the beautiful children they would one day have together...

And, unbeknownst to her, all of it *had* been a complete figment of her imagination, with no hope of any of it ever coming true.

She had to be completely insane even to think of going out to dinner with Ethan.

He had well and truly crushed every one of her romantically girlish dreams—this man had already made a fool of her once, taken her love, made love to her, before breaking her heart in so many pieces it had never completely been put back together again.

It had taken Mia years to get over her complete distrust of men—if she had!—but even now she still compared every man she met to Ethan Black. Not tall enough. Not dark-haired enough. Not ruggedly handsome enough. Not muscular enough. Not jungle-cat-lean enough. Not sexy enough. Not funny enough. Just not *Ethan* enough!

How sad was that? The man had used her, deceived her, pretended to care for her for his own ends—ends that he had now achieved without any help from her— and yet just being with him again like this was enough for Mia to know she still wanted him...

'Turn the car around, Ethan!'

'What...?' Ethan's concentration on the road and traffic in front of him shifted sideways onto Mia as he gave her a brief searching glance. He could see how pale her face was by the streetlights, her eyes a huge and haunted green.

Those eyes were turned towards him, and yet at the same time seemed to look straight through him. 'Turn the car around and take me home.'

'But—'

'I'm not doing this, Ethan,' she told him flatly.

He turned his attention back to the road ahead, his jaw tight. 'You have to eat.'

Mia gave a humourless laugh. 'We both know I'm not talking about eating.'

'Then what *are* we talking about?'

He knew! He *had* to know! There was no way Ethan couldn't be as aware as Mia of the sexual tension that literally seemed to hang in the air in the close confines of the sports car!

It surrounded them like an invisible cloak. Tense. Alive. Always thrumming beneath the surface—just as it had every time they were together.

'Please take me home, Ethan,' Mia repeated firmly.

'No.' His hands tightened about the steering wheel as he pushed his foot down and the car accelerated rather than slowed down.

'I said—'

'I heard what you said, Mia.' He shot her another sharp glance before as quickly turning away from the accusation he could read in her eyes. 'And whatever nonsense is buzzing around in your head this time I suggest you get rid of it. Because we are going to sit down and eat dinner. And while we do so we're going to talk like the rational human beings we both are.'

'You think?' she came back bleakly.

Ethan gave a shrug. 'I live in hope, yes!' he said wearily.

Whatever Mia had been thinking about this past few minutes it hadn't been pleasant. The problem was, none of the thoughts she had about him seemed to be pleasant ones!

Ethan might not have liked the things Mia had believed of him five years ago, but in a way he had understood them. Even before his mother's relationship with William became public the strikes against him had been pretty damning. He worked for her father. Not only was Mia a wealthy young woman in her own right, but she was also her father's only heir.

And yet none of those things had come into play the night Ethan had seen her again at that company party— not where and for whom he worked, nor who Mia was. They hadn't seemed important in the months that followed either, during those days and nights when they were together constantly. Talking, laughing, loving...

But convincing Mia of that had been pretty much a non-starter once the scandal of her mother's suicide and his mother and her father's relationship broke in the media. It was no more likely now; you had to trust someone in order to believe in them—and Mia had shown Ethan time and time again that she no longer trusted him to tell her the correct time of day!

So what was he doing by insisting she go out to dinner with him? A dinner that would torturous at best, and agonisingly uncomfortable at worst?

Besides which, was a public restaurant really the place for the conversation he wanted to have—needed to have—with Mia this evening?

The answer to that was a definite no!

He had allowed himself to become sidetracked by Mia's insistence that she wouldn't have dinner with him.

Had forgotten, in the battle of wills that ensued, the whole purpose of his being here this evening.

'Okay, Mia, you win.' Ethan slowed the car before making a totally illegal U-turn in the middle of the road, much to the noisily expressed annoyance of the other drivers on both sides of the road.

'Ethan…!' Mia gave an incredulous laugh as several rude gestures came their way to accompany the loud tooting of car horns. 'Are you completely insane?'

'Probably.' Ethan grinned at her in the illumination given off by the street lights. 'This was what you wanted, wasn't it?'

It had been, yes. But now that Ethan had actually given her what she wanted Mia contrarily wished that he hadn't. Which was pretty stupid. Masochistic. And that didn't begin to cover the contradiction of feelings that now assailed her.

Relief?

Disappointment?

Relief at the two of them being spared the ordeal of trying to be polite to each other in a public restaurant.

Disappointment because she knew that Ethan would no doubt leave as soon as he had dropped her off at her apartment.

She hadn't actually *wanted* to spend the evening with Ethan—had she?

Hadn't this man already hurt her enough for a lifetime? Hadn't he—? Oh, to hell with it! 'I have some chicken at home I was going to cook for my dinner tonight, if you're interested?'

Ethan shot her a narrow-eyed glance. 'Are you inviting me to share it?' he finally said slowly.

'It did sound that way, yes…' Mia acknowledged reluctantly.

Ethan gave a disbelieving shake of his head as he slowed and then parked his car at the coffee shop before turning in his seat to look at her. 'And you wonder why I've never married! I prefer certainty in my life rather than instability, and women—all women—are just too damned unpredictable,' he added at her questioning glance.

'Makes us interesting, though,' she came back dryly.

'That's one word for it!'

'Well?' Mia said once more, only just stopping herself from squirming in discomfort as Ethan continued to study her carefully. Not surprisingly. Her behaviour was completely erratic—one moment rejecting his company altogether and the next inviting him into her home for dinner!

What on earth did she think the outcome of spending an evening with Ethan could possibly be? She and Ethan had become enemies the day she'd learnt of his widowed mother's relationship with her married father, and nothing either of them said or did was ever going to change that.

'Too late for second thoughts now, Mia,' Ethan drawled as he obviously saw those doubts in her expression. He got out of the car before coming round and opening the passenger door for her. 'There's something I need to…discuss with you this evening, anyway.'

'What is it?' Mia frowned slightly as she got out of the car to stand beside Ethan on the pavement, at the same time looking for her keys in her oversized handbag.

'It would be better if we talked inside.' Ethan took the keys from her hand before placing a hand firmly beneath her elbow and walking her to the door at the back of the coffee shop.

'Ethan…?'

Ethan regretted the tension he could hear in Mia's tone now. She had already known too much unhappiness in her twenty-five years, and although Ethan still couldn't approve of the way she had cut her father—and him—out her life, he could at least acknowledge that she had found a degree of peace in the running of her coffee shop.

A peace and contentment he knew he was about to destroy…

He turned the key in the lock and ushered Mia inside, to close the door firmly behind them before handing the keys back to her. 'Do you have any wine to go with the chicken?'

'Do I need to have…?'

'It wouldn't do any harm.'

She gave a pained frown. 'I have some white wine, yes.'

'Then I suggest we open a bottle or two and have a glass or six.' He nodded grimly in the direction of the stairs leading up to her apartment.

Mia looked even more wary as she began to walk up the stairs. 'That bad, hmm?'

Probably, Ethan acknowledged as he followed a short distance behind her. He should have realised there was no easy way he could do this—that his teasing earlier, the idea of taking Mia out to dinner, would ultimately make no difference to the shock he was about to deliver.

He could put it off for a few days' more. Didn't *have* to have this conversation with Mia now…

'Okay, Ethan.' Mia handed him one of the two glasses of white wine she had poured as he stood lost in thought in the doorway of her small kitchen. 'What do you want to talk about?'

'This apartment is a little…small, isn't it?'

'After living in a mansion—several mansions all over the world—until I was twenty, you mean?' she retorted.

'Well…yes.' He grimaced.

Mia shrugged. 'I've been happier here than I ever was in any of those places.'

'But surely you don't bake in here?' He frowned at the smallness of the kitchen.

The pine kitchen *was* compact, Mia acknowledged, only really big enough for one person to move about in comfortably. And, as Ethan had pointed out, it was certainly not big enough for the amount of baking Mia did on a daily basis. All of which was a total irrelevance…

'I use the industrial equipment in the kitchen downstairs,' she dismissed. 'And delaying answering me isn't going to sugar-coat whatever the pill is, Ethan!'

No, it wasn't, Ethan accepted heavily. He just wished he didn't have to do this. That there was some other way.

Mia's stubborn refusal even to discuss seeing William again meant there *was* no other way! She had given Ethan no choice but to do what he was about to do. Even if he might wish it could be otherwise.

He drew in a harsh breath. 'I need to talk to you about the reason for your father's heart attack—'

'I think you had better leave after all, Ethan,' she cut in quickly.

Ethan stood firm in the doorway. 'I'm not going anywhere until we've talked this through.'

'Then I will!' Her eyes flashed darkly as she brushed past him. 'Go away, Ethan,' she said dully as he followed her through to the adjoining sitting room.

A stylish and yet comfortable room, its walls were

painted a pale cream. There was a deep peach-coloured carpet, paler peach sofa and chairs, and light pine furniture. The prints on the walls reflected that colour scheme.

Ethan took all of this in at a glance, before his attention focused on the defensive woman who stood so tense and pale beside the unlit fireplace, drinking her wine as she met his gaze with fearless challenge.

Mia had never looked more beautiful!

That wispy golden hair was like a halo about the angles and hollows of Mia's face, that sinuously graceful body—pert breasts, slender waist, curvaceous thighs—tensed as if for a fight.

Ethan determinedly dampened down that stirring desire as his mouth firmed with new resolve. 'Whether you like it or not, we *do* have to talk about William's heart attack.'

'I don't have to talk to you about anything, Ethan. Least of all my father,' Mia told him with scornful dismissal.

'Yes—you—do.'

'You can insist all you like, Ethan, but it will ultimately make no difference,' she said calmly. 'I just don't want to hear anything you have to say on that subject.'

'I didn't want it to be like this—' Ethan gave a frustrated shake of his head. 'Maybe I should just show you?' He reached into the breast pocket of his jacket.

Mia eyed him warily now. 'Show me what?'

'I have some photographs—'

'More? Are they something different this time? I'm really not in the mood to look at happy-ever-after snaps from the family album, Ethan!'

'There's nothing in the least happy-ever-after about these photographs.' He held an envelope in his hand now, knuckles showing white as he gripped that envelope tightly.

Mia's tension increased as she looked at Ethan searchingly and saw the grimness of his expression and the regret in those otherwise chilling grey eyes. Her hand shook slightly as she took another hesitant sip of her wine before answering him. 'What do you have in there, Ethan?' she prompted slowly, eyeing the envelope as if it were a bomb about to go off.

Which, considering Ethan's obvious tension, might indeed prove to be the case...

His expression became even grimmer. 'Did you read in the newspapers six months ago, or see on the news, that a woman's body was found in a ditch in Cornwall?'

Mia rarely watched television, but she vaguely recalled reading something about that in the newspapers—yes, the badly decomposed body of a young woman had been found in a ditch but and remained unidentified for several weeks while the police continued their investigation.

Mia raised her stricken gaze to look sharply across the room at Ethan. 'Are you telling me—? Is it possible that my father may have thought—'

'Yes,' Ethan confirmed heavily. 'As soon as he saw the news on the television William contacted the police, explained the situation of your disappearance almost five years earlier, and asked if he could see the body.'

Mia felt herself sway dizzily. 'And they *let* him...?'

'No, they refused to allow that—wanted positive proof from dental records before they would allow anyone to view the body,' Ethan bit out grimly. 'But William, being William, wouldn't let it go, and he eventually managed—don't ask me how!—to acquire some photographs he could look at.'

Her gaze returned as if mesmerised to the envelope Ethan held so tightly in his hand. 'And that's them?'

'Some of them, yes.' Ethan nodded abruptly. 'Of course they proved by dental records a couple of days later that it was the body of someone else, but for over twenty-four hours William was left with the terrible thought that it might be you.'

'Let me see the photographs, Ethan.'

'Now that you're at least listening to me there's no reason for you to upset yourself by looking at them.'

'Don't.' Mia stopped Ethan as he would have put the envelope back in his pocket, putting her glass carefully down onto the glass-topped coffee table before holding out her hand. 'Give me the envelope, Ethan.' Her gaze was very clear and very determined as it met his. 'I want to see what my father saw.'

'There's no need for this, Mia—'

'If, as you seem to be implying, they were the reason for my father's heart attack, then I believe there's every need.'

'He collapsed only half an hour after looking at them—so, yes, I think we can safely assume it was the shock of thinking you were dead that triggered it.' Ethan could still clearly remember his own shocked disbelief and pain as they had waited for confirmation as to whether or not the woman in those photographs was Mia...

Mia felt slightly numb, and yet at the same time her thoughts were crystal-clear: if what Ethan said was true—and he could have no reason to lie to her when what he said could so easily be disproved—then, as Ethan had claimed yesterday, her disappearance really *had* been the reason for her father's heart attack six months ago...

'I want to see them.' Her gaze remained steady on Ethan's as she continued to hold out her hand. 'I *need* to see them, Ethan.' Her voice shook despite her determination. 'Please.'

It was hearing that break in Mia's voice—the first crack Ethan had detected in the walls she had built about her emotions this past five years—that finally gave Ethan hope that she might still care something for William after all.

He grimaced. 'They really aren't pleasant,' he warned grimly as he reluctantly handed her the envelope.

Ethan watched warily as she opened it and slid out the half a dozen photographs inside before looking down. A single glance at the top photograph was enough to drain all the colour from her cheeks, her skin actually seemed to turn a sickly grey as she quickly flicked through the rest of the photographs before allowing them to slip from her fingers to fall unheeded to the carpeted floor.

'Damn it to hell…!' Ethan stepped forward.

'Ethan, unless you want me to be sick all over you, I suggest you get out of my way!' Mia warned between gritted teeth.

One look at the green tinge to her cheeks was enough to make Ethan step aside, his face grim, as he watched Mia almost run out of the sitting room and into a room further down the hallway—obviously the bathroom—before closing the door and locking it firmly behind her.

Not that Ethan could blame her—he'd had the same reaction himself the first time he'd looked at those photographs and thought that it was Mia…

CHAPTER SIX

IT DIDN'T take Mia long to dispose of the contents of her stomach—she had been too busy in the coffee shop today to have time to eat properly, and obviously hadn't had dinner yet. Which was probably as well in the circumstances.

The photographs Ethan had shown her were—they were—

Oh, God, how must her father have felt? How would any parent feel when faced with such horrific images of a—a thing that might once have been their child? If her father had believed even briefly that young woman's body might be her—

'Are you okay, Mia?' A soft knock on the door accompanied Ethan's concerned query.

Was she okay? She had just been physically ill after being so horrified by those photographs. And she was still horrified at the thought of her father having looked at those images and believing for even one moment that it might be her.

As Ethan had intended she should be?

'Mia?' There was no missing the strain in Ethan's voice.

Mia straightened with determination. 'I'm fine, Ethan,' she answered firmly as she moved to the sink to throw cold water on her face before brushing her teeth, her hands shaking slightly. Her reflection in the mirror over the sink showed that her eyes were darkly shadowed and her face sickly pale.

She still had no idea what she wanted to do about seeing her father again—couldn't even think straight enough at the moment to come up with a logical answer to that question. In fact she didn't want to think at all right now. She, needed—needed—

'Mia, if you don't open this door immediately I'm going to kick it down!' Ethan warned impatiently.

She needed a complete diversion from everything that had happened here so far this evening!

Mia felt calm, and her hands were no longer trembling as she unlocked and opened the door to look up at Ethan. He had obviously been running agitated fingers through the short thickness of his hair. Several dark strands were falling across his forehead, tempting Mia into wanting to reach up and brush those silky locks off his brow.

'Mia…?' He eyed her uncertainly as she stood unmoving in the doorway. 'Can I get you anything? Some more wine? Maybe chocolate? I seem to remember they were the things you wanted when you were upset…'

Yes, they had been. Whenever university work had seemed daunting, when worry over her mother, or anything else had bothered her, Mia had always turned to chocolate or wine—or both—to ward off that worry.

That Ethan remembered that too was disconcerting…

Ethan gave a pained wince as looked down at her. 'I apologise. I shouldn't have used those shock tactics—' He stopped speaking as Mia placed her fingertips across his lips. 'You don't want me to apologise…?' He eyed her guardedly.

She gave a brief smile. 'Oh, I do, Ethan. I'm just not interested in verbal apologies at the moment.'

He became very still, his gaze guarded as he looked down at her searchingly. Her eyes were a clear and direct green as she returned his gaze unflinchingly.

'How about a non-verbal one?' he said slowly. 'I seem to remember there was a third thing that always succeeded in distracting you...' he added huskily. 'Unless you think it would be inappropriate right now...?'

Was that uncertainty Mia heard in Ethan's voice? Surely not. The Ethan she had known in the past had never seemed uncertain of anything—this more mature and forcefully arrogant Ethan even less so.

Mia moistened her lips before answering. 'Why don't we try it and see...?'

Ethan's steely gaze remained fixed on her face, the tension leaving his body as he was reassured by whatever he saw there. 'Sitting room or bedroom?'

Mia's stomach did a somersault at the enormity of what she was doing. 'The sitting room, please.' Even to her own ears she sounded slightly breathless.

Ethan stepped back into the hallway. 'Shall we...?' he prompted gruffly.

Mia's stomach gave another lurch. She really had no idea what she was doing. Only knew that right now she badly needed the feel of Ethan's hands on her...

'Ooh, that is *sooo* good...'

'More?'

'Yes...'

'Harder?'

'Yes, please. Oh, God... That is truly wonderful! I'd forgotten just how good you are at this,' Mia added achingly.

Only a table lamp illuminated the room as Ethan stood behind the sofa, with Mia sitting in front of him, and continued to knead the knots of tension from her nape and between her shoulderblades, his fingers digging into the soft wool of her sweater as he massaged just firmly enough to ease that tension.

Of course he would have preferred it if Mia had been completely naked and lying on a bed while his hands massaged and soothed her bared and creamy flesh, but after the shock she had suffered when he had handed her those photographs he accepted that beggars couldn't be choosers.

Just touching Mia at all was pleasurable. Ethan could feel the delicacy of her bones beneath the softness of flesh, and the heat she generated. The soft allure of her feminine perfume was permeating his senses. As for what her groans of pleasure were doing to his own body...

Ethan physically ached. That ache was becoming a pulsing need as Mia continued to give those little cries of pleasure as he massaged her back and shoulders. Cries of pleasure like those he could so easily remember her making during their lovemaking.

'Don't stop, Ethan.' Mia's voice was husky as she turned to look at him from beneath long silky lashes.

Ethan didn't want to stop. What he wanted was to go so much further, deeper—hell, he was so aroused now he felt as if he was going to explode. An arousal that would no doubt result in Mia asking him to leave if she were to realize.

'Ethan...?'

'Right.' He gave a self-derisive shake of his head as he once again ran soothing—caressing—fingers over the softness of her shoulders and nape. The shortness of

Mia's hair shone golden in the glow of the table lamp, revealing a soft and vulnerable nape, and a tiny, kissable mole just beneath her right earlobe. The change in the way Mia responded to his caressing hands was so subtle Ethan almost missed it. Almost didn't notice the way her neck now arched sinuously, the increased heat of her skin through the wool of her sweater...

Ethan's own breathing became shallow and uneven as he changed the direction of his caresses, his fingers now moving slowly, lightly against the creaminess of Mia's neck. Her head fell back against the sofa, her eyes closing as Ethan touched the delicate arch of her throat, seeking out those sensitive hollows before moving lower. His hands stilled, and he was waiting for Mia to protest as he gently cupped the firm thrust of her breasts.

Breasts that a single touch revealed were completely naked beneath the wool of Mia's sweater, their softness tipped with nipples that Ethan knew from experience were the colour of raspberries—and just as succulent to the taste...

'Mia—'

'Don't talk, Ethan, please,' she groaned, eyes still closed as Ethan leant over the back of the sofa to look down into her face.

There was no missing the flush of arousal to Mia's cheeks, the soft rose of her lips. And those lips were moist and slightly parted, as if in invitation.

Ethan knew he should resist that invitation. Mia had been deeply disturbed by those photographs—and still was? There were still so many misunderstandings between the two of them—so many things that hadn't yet been said.

And Ethan didn't give a damn about a single one of

those things as his head lowered to claim Mia's lips with his own!

Mia didn't move, eyes remaining firmly closed as her lips parted in acceptance of Ethan's kiss.

A wonderful expectant warmth had surged through Mia's body minutes ago at the first touch of Ethan's fingers. That warmth had quickly spread, causing her breasts to become hot and aching even as that heat simmered and settled achingly between her thighs. That heat expanded now as Ethan kissed her, his deft and knowledgeable fingers caressing her nipples, lightly squeezing the aching tips at the same time as his tongue moved between her parted lips.

Mia responded to that intimacy by thrusting back as her arms moved up about Ethan's muscled shoulders and her fingers became entangled in the dark thickness of the hair at his nape. Only the sound of their ragged breathing broke the expectant silence that now surrounded them.

Mia knew she had wanted this, craved this, since first seeing Ethan again yesterday—that a part of her had instantly begun to wonder, to question if this older, more forceful Ethan and the more mature and self-confident Mia would be as physically combustible together as the more youthful Ethan and Mia had been five years ago.

If anything, they were more so!

Their lips parted hungrily, tongues duelling as Mia turned in Ethan's arms to kneel up on the sofa, her aching breasts now pressed against the hardness of his chest as his arms slid about her waist and his hands moved caressingly underneath her sweater to touch the heated flesh beneath.

Ethan kissed Mia hungrily, deeply, as he revelled in touching the silky softness of her skin before pushing up the barrier of her sweater completely, to bare the slender curve of her spine and the firm thrust of her breasts.

Mia groaned low in protest as Ethan broke that kiss, her groan turning to an aching sigh of pleasure as one of Ethan's hands moved to cup beneath her breast before he lowered his head and ran his tongue over one bared nipple, tasting her, pleasuring her, gently circling, then taking her fully into his mouth, his other hand pressed firmly against her spine.

Mia's breath was a painful rasp, and her fingers were clinging to Ethan's shoulders as the pleasure washed over her in waves. She became aware of the warmth pouring off Ethan, of the heat of arousal hanging heavy in the air between them.

Ethan shifted his attention to her other breast, his hand now moving down the slender slope of her belly and then lower. The soft pad of his palm pressed against her, moving rhythmically, driving Mia's pleasure to another level.

Mia's neck arched back. 'Oh, God…! I want—I need—'

His breath was a warm caress against her breast as he released her to look up at her with glittering eyes. 'More?'

'Yes!'

'Harder?'

'God, yes…'

Mia didn't care that this was a teasing repeat of their earlier conversation. She just wanted, *needed* Ethan to satisfy the torturous desire coursing through her body.

He blew softly against the tip of her damp breast as his hand moved to the fastening of her jeans. Just that light caress was enough to make Mia tremble uncontrollably.

Ethan pushed Mia's trousers down her thighs to reveal she wore only a tiny pair of black lace panties beneath. He felt the dampness between her legs. In readiness for him...

The blood was pounding through Ethan's veins with every rapid beat of his heart. His breathing was a harsh rasp in his throat as his hand dipped beneath that black lace to touch her, before the soft pad of his thumb began a slow and rhythmic caress.

He felt Mia moving into his caress as his mouth once again found her hardened nipple, felt Mia's pleasure as she moved ever closer to climax.

Ethan drew his breath in sharply as Mia's hands moved beneath his polo shirt to touch his chest and the flatness of his stomach, those delicately light fingers lingering at the fastening of his jeans before moving lower, her palm pressing against the rigid length of his erection.

Had Ethan ever been this aroused before?

So hard and wanting he could feel himself on the edge of release just at the hard press of those fingers against him?

Ethan didn't think so—knew he hadn't as Mia moved her hand against him.

She shifted, legs parting, before letting out a low and keening cry as her body convulsed and contracted against Ethan as she rode the surging orgasm to mindless completion.

It seemed an eternity later when Mia allowed her head to drop down weakly to rest on Ethan's shoulder as her release reached a slow and shuddering halt.

Which was when the full force of what she had just encouraged to happen washed over her...

Her breasts felt hot and heavy from the attentions of

Ethan's mouth and hands. The force of her explosive release was still in the air.

Mia's release.

Not Ethan's.

Her hand still resting against him told her of his ready arousal...

Mia had been a virgin the first time she and Ethan had made love together five years ago—inexperienced, physically shy. But even in her innocence she had never been a selfish lover. She had certainly never taken her own pleasure and left Ethan achingly unsatisfied!

'Mia?'

She couldn't look at Ethan now—was absolutely mortified by her behaviour. She had more or less demanded that Ethan make love to her—oh, he'd had the option of refusing, but what man would?—and had then taken her pleasure without thought of— 'I'm sorry.'

'You're *sorry*?' he repeated forcefully. 'What the hell does that mean?'

'I was upset—not thinking straight. But that was still no reason for me to...' Mia gave a shake of her head. 'It was still no reason for me to—'

'For you to do what, Mia?' Ethan prompted impatiently. 'Exactly what happened just now?'

She wished she knew! Oh, she *had* been upset—and definitely not thinking straight—but was that really an acceptable explanation for using Ethan in that way? The logical part of Mia's brain had told her that it was madness for her even to be attracted to Ethan, let alone ever allow herself to feel anything for him again. The illogical part wondered, after her uncontrollable response just now, if those feelings for Ethan had ever stopped...

Something she definitely didn't want to think about right now!

Instead she moved up on the sofa, holding Ethan's gaze with her own as her hands moved to the fastening of his jeans once more.

'What do you think you're doing?' Ethan's hands moved to capture and hold hers.

Colour warmed her cheeks as she looked up at him. 'You didn't— Haven't—' She gave a shrug. 'I was just going to—'

'I can guess what you were just going to do, Mia!' he ground out harshly, stepping away from her. 'Thanks— but, no thanks,' he snapped coldly.

'What do you mean…?'

'I mean that particular moment has passed,' he rasped harshly. 'And I'm not about to use you for sex as you obviously used me!'

Mia moved sharply away, her hands dropping back to her sides as she pulled her sweater down over her exposed breasts and fastened her denims before kneeling back on her heels to look up at him. Ethan's face was all hard and unapproachable angles in the lamplight, his expression harshly uncompromising.

Her wince was pained. 'That was unbelievably crude, Ethan.'

'I prefer to think of it as being realistic.' His eyes glittered that opaque, unreadable silver as he looked down at her through narrowed lids, his jaw tense, a nerve pulsing at the base of his throat.

Her cheeks had gone very pale. 'I've offered—'

'I'm well aware of what you've offered, Mia,' he snapped. 'And, as I said, I've lost the inclination.' He continued remorselessly, 'But, if it makes you feel better, you can owe me, okay?' he added insultingly.

She blinked. 'Owe you…?'

Ethan nodded abruptly. 'The next time I'm in the mood for some uncomplicated sex I know who to come to.'

If Ethan was meaning to humiliate her then he had succeeded. Mia's cheeks burned with embarrassment.

'I made a mistake—there's no need to be so deliberately hurtful...'

As far as Ethan was concerned there was every need!

He should have known when Mia cautioned him earlier—'Don't talk, Ethan...'—that making love with Mia tonight was all wrong. That as far as she was concerned it hadn't been Ethan Black making love to her at all. He was just some faceless, nameless man with whom she could use sex to force the horrific images of those photographs from her mind.

Ethan backed off. 'I think it's time I left.' Past time, if he were truthful.

'Yes.'

Quite where the two of them went after tonight Ethan had no idea. Although he suspected that on a personal basis he and Mia were going precisely nowhere. Which in no way nullified the reason he had come here tonight.

'You still haven't told me what you intend doing about your father.'

Mia stood up to turn away from his piercing gaze as she straightened her clothing, totally aware as she did so that this was far from her finest hour. Ethan was right. She *had* used him just now—and in the worst possible way. And to make matters worse she had compounded that initial mistake with their that ridiculous attempt to return the favour!

'Or maybe you just intend letting William continue to

believe you might be dead in another ditch somewhere?' Ethan accused.

Mia's eyes flashed her anger. 'I have absolutely no idea yet what I'm going to do about that situation, okay?' And she truly didn't…

The thought of her father looking at the remains of that poor woman in those awful photographs and fearing it might be her was truly awful. But, awful as it was, Mia knew that none of that changed the things that still stood between the two of them. Namely her mother's suicide five years ago, and the revelation of her father's relationship with Grace Black…

Her frown deepened. 'I need time to think about this some more before deciding.'

'And in the meantime you intend to let your father continue to suffer?'

Her chin rose at Ethan's deepening contempt for her. 'I'm not stopping you from telling him you've seen me—'

'I believe I stated yesterday where I stand in regard to having anyone telling me what I can or cannot do!' Ethan dismissed harshly.

Yesterday.

Was it really only just over twenty-four hours since she had first seen Ethan again? It seemed so much longer. Mia felt years older, not hours!

She gave a shaky sigh. 'As I said, you are perfectly at liberty to tell my father—'

'Oh, no, Mia. You don't wriggle out of this that easily,' Ethan cut in scathingly. 'I'm not your errand boy. If you want William to know you're still alive, then you can damn well tell him so yourself.'

She glared her frustration. 'Maybe I'll decide to do just that!'

'When?'

'When I'm good and ready!'

'If you ever are.'

She drew in a sharp breath. 'Stop pushing me, Ethan! I've already told you I haven't decided what I'm going to do about my father. When I do you'll be the first to know, okay?'

'No, it's not okay,' Ethan rasped. 'I was right about you yesterday—you really have turned into a cold and selfish little witch, haven't you?' he added disgustedly as he strode over to the door.

Mia's hand shook as she carefully picked up her glass of wine from the coffee table where she had placed it earlier, taking several soothing sips as she willed herself to hold it together until Ethan had gone. She couldn't break down in front of Ethan. She couldn't let him see—

'Oh, and Mia…?' Ethan turned to stand in the open doorway.

She looked across at him warily. 'Yes…?'

'Just so that you know…' He stepped out into the hallway. 'It may take months—*years*—but I always collect on my debts!'

Mia didn't even hesitate as she lifted her arm and threw the glass across the room at him.

Ethan stepped neatly in the hallway and pushed the door closed behind him. 'Missed…' he murmured, loud enough for her to hear, before he went down the stairs. The outside door closed behind him seconds later.

Mia looked over to where the wine glass had shattered against the closed door, numb as she looked at the broken glass all over the floor and the rivulets of wine dripping down the wood.

She burst into loud and inconsolable tears. Tears that owed absolutely nothing to the mess she was going to have to clear up once she stopped crying, and everything to do with the dark-haired, silver-eyed man who was wreaking total havoc in her life for the second time.

CHAPTER SEVEN

'THANKS, Trish,' Ethan drawled softly as his secretary showed Mia into his office at eleven o'clock the following Monday morning, waiting until the other woman had left the room before turning to look at Mia as she crossed the room to stand in front of his desk.

The high heels on her black shoes were complimentary to the visible length of her shapely legs, but the black business suit and pale green blouse Mia was wearing today made her look as if she were paying a visit to her bank manager rather than the man who had once been her lover.

Who was still her lover…?

Ethan had been absolutely furious when he'd left Mia's apartment on Friday evening. Not just with Mia, but with himself too—for allowing things to get as out of control between them as they obviously had, and so further complicating a situation that was complex enough already.

It hadn't helped that Ethan had then spent the whole weekend remembering making love to Mia—his constant state of arousal at those memories even making him regret that he had stopped her when she had attempted to return the favour.

Mia had been a generous and responsive lover

five years ago, but the woman Ethan had held in his arms, made love to on Friday evening, had been exactly that: a woman. Bolder. More self-confident. More experienced?

Every time Ethan thought that might be the case he felt his rage deepening. Which was ridiculous. Mia was twenty-five now, and it would be extremely naive on Ethan's part to think she wouldn't have taken other lovers during the past five years. Even if the thought of some other man touching her in the intimate way he had did make him green with envy!

To arrive at his office at nine o'clock this morning and learn that Mia had already telephoned and made an appointment to see him at eleven o'clock today hadn't improved his mood in the slightest, and he was left wondering exactly what it was she wanted to talk to him about.

'I'm waiting, Mia,' he reminded her tersely now, as she made no attempt to start the conversation.

Mia was well aware Ethan was waiting for her to say something. Just as she could tell by his coolly remote expression that he wasn't about to make this in the least easy for her.

It had been a very long weekend—hours and hours when Mia had determinedly put Friday evening, and Ethan, from her mind, and instead worked in the coffee shop on Saturday and then spent Sunday baking from morning until night as she went over and over again in her mind what her options were concerning her father.

Ethan's refusal to tell William he had spoken to her, and that she was alive and well and living in London, appeared to leave Mia with only two choices: refuse to see her father again, or agree to visit him.

To refuse would not only leave Mia feeling guilt-ridden, but also uneasy that one day Ethan might change his mind and tell her father where she was anyway.

Seeing her father again would, Mia felt sure, result in yet more heartache for both of them. She wasn't ready to forgive William for the past—wasn't sure she ever would be—in which case, apart from reassuring her father that she was indeed still alive and not in a ditch somewhere, as Ethan had suggested William might think she was, Mia couldn't see what good it would do either of them to meet again.

And yet every time she so much as thought of that poor woman who had been found dead six months ago, of her father looking at those photographs and believing for even a short time that it might be her, all Mia's previous logic went completely out of the window. Ethan had several times accused her of being cold and selfish, but Mia knew she was neither of those things—that beneath the anger she still felt towards her father she also still loved him...

How she now felt towards Ethan was less clear to her!

Much as Mia had tried not to think about him over the weekend, she knew she hadn't completely succeeded. As she'd lain in her bed this past three nights, attempting to fall asleep, the memories of their lovemaking had come back to haunt her. Just the memory of Ethan's hands and lips on her body was enough to arouse her all over again!

'You may have all day to waste, Mia, but I have another appointment at eleven-thirty,' Ethan stated, and gave a pointed glance at the thin gold watch on his left wrist.

Mia straightened. 'I've decided—after careful consideration I've decided to see my father.' The words came out in an awkward rush.

'Really?' he murmured softly.

'Yes—really,' she confirmed irritably. Damn it, Ethan might show a little more enthusiasm when this was what he had been pushing for her to do.

Instead he relaxed back in his chair, dark brows raised over sceptical grey eyes. 'And you've come here to tell me that because...?'

'Because I expect you to arrange the meeting, of course,' Mia said irritably. 'And don't say "Really?" again, in that sarcastic tone,' she continued impatiently as Ethan continued to look at her from between narrowed lids. 'We both know that my just turning up on the doorstep of my father's villa in the South of France is likely to do more harm than good.'

Yes, Ethan conceded ruefully, that was something they could both agree on.

And maybe Mia agreeing to see William after all proved that she wasn't as changed, as cold and selfish as Ethan had believed that she was. Maybe. But it was still only a maybe.

He had briefly thought he had reached the old Mia— the warm and affectionate Mia—on Friday evening. Her physical response to him was as strong as it had ever been. As his had been to her. Until her own behaviour had made it so obvious that she had only wanted some distraction...

Ethan's mouth tightened and he straightened behind his desk.

'You're serious about this?'

'Yes.'

'How serious?'

Her eyes flashed her impatience with his scepticism. 'I'm here, aren't I?'

Oh, yes, Mia was here. One of the Mias, at least. A businesslike Mia that Ethan didn't know at all. He nodded tersely. 'In that case I'll organise a flight to the South of France for later this afternoon.'

'But—I can't go today!' Mia gasped.

'Why not?' he prompted calmly.

'I— Well— Because I'm not ready to go yet! And when I am ready I can organise my own flight, thank you very much. I just need you to—'

'Burton Industries has its own small jet now, Mia.'

She blinked. 'I didn't realise that...'

Ethan shrugged. 'It's more comfortable for William to have his own plane.'

'Even so, I can't just disappear to the South of France this afternoon. I have a business to run—'

'The coffee shop isn't open on Mondays.'

Mia didn't need to ask how he knew that; Ethan had obviously memorised that report on her before shredding it! 'That's beside the point—'

'What *is* the point, Mia?' Ethan stood up abruptly to move around the desk, his eyes hardening to a steely grey as Mia instinctively took a step away from him. As if she were frightened of being anywhere near him, damn it.

Or as if she were frightened of her reaction to his close proximity...?

Ethan eyed her in consideration; Mia's green eyes were wide and wary in the paleness of her face—her body was tensed as if for flight, her hands clenched at her sides.

'No need to look so nervous, Mia.' Ethan gave a rueful smile as he leant back against his desk and folded his arms across his chest, looking down at her with mocking eyes. 'I would prefer to be somewhere a little more comfortable than my office when I collect on my debt. Preferably somewhere with the luxury of a bed...'

Mia drew her breath in sharply even as she felt the warmth of colour flood her cheeks. 'I came here to talk about my father, Ethan, not to play games with you!'

He gave a cool nod of his head. 'And I've already suggested arranging to fly to the South of France this afternoon.'

'I—'

'For two reasons,' Ethan continued. 'One, it doesn't give you a chance to change your mind.' He eyed her knowingly. 'And two, I believe William has already spent enough years worrying and missing you.'

Mia gave a pained frown as she easily heard the rebuke in Ethan's tone. 'I'm sure my father has been far too busy with you and your mother in his life to really notice my absence.'

Ethan continued to look at her intently. 'William loves my mother very much, and I'm sure he is fond of me, but neither of us could ever be—or indeed would ever want to be—considered as a replacement for his own daughter.'

Mia gave a shake of her head. 'I think you're exaggerating, Ethan. I look so much like the wife he had so obviously fallen out of love with long before she died that I would only have been a constant reminder of that failed marriage.'

'You can't seriously believe that?' Ethan looked at her incredulously.

'Why can't I?' Mia began to pace restlessly.

'Because it's ridiculous to think that an innocent child can be held responsible for its parents' failings.'

Mia eyed him derisively. 'And who told you *that* little gem of wisdom?'

'My mother, as it happens,' he murmured with a frown. 'And I don't believe for one moment that William thinks of you in that way any more than my mother ever has in regard to me.'

She stopped pacing to look across at him. 'What do you mean?'

He gave a humourless smile. 'Maybe if we hadn't spent so much time in bed together five years ago, but had talked a little too, you would already know what I mean.'

'Ethan…!' She eyed him exasperatedly.

He gave a shrug. 'My own father was an unpredictable drunk and a bully.' Ethan gave an acknowledging inclination of his head as Mia gave a surprised gasp. 'To a degree that he made almost the whole twelve years my mother was married to him, and the first ten years of my own life, nothing but a misery.'

'He—was he physically abusive?'

Ethan shook his head. 'It was more emotional and mental cruelty. Probably as a sop to the fact that his wife was more successful as a deputy headmistress, as she was at the time, than he as the car salesman he was.'

Mia swallowed hard. 'How did he die?'

'He just stroked out whilst in the midst of a drunken rage because my mother had called to say she was going to be late arriving home from work one evening.'

'I—were you with him?'

Ethan's gaze was very direct. 'As it happens, yes.'

Mia had never known about any of this in Ethan's past. 'I'm sorry…'

'Why should you be sorry?' he asked dryly.

'I—well, I've never asked you about your father…'

Ethan shrugged. 'I never bothered to talk to you about him.'

Mia was very aware that the reason for this oversight was because for the three months they had been together she and Ethan had been so totally physically engrossed in each other that they had rarely talked about anything.

As for Grace Black…

Tall and strikingly beautiful, with rich auburn hair and lively blue eyes, as the headmistress of Southlands School Grace Black had always given the impression of cool and unruffled elegance; Mia would never have guessed she had been married for twelve years to the man Ethan had described. Ethan's own father…

'I look just like him,' Ethan continued evenly. 'Same build. Same dark hair. Same grey eyes.' He gave a dismissive shrug. 'It's never stopped my mother from seeing me for exactly who I am rather than who and what my father was.'

Because Ethan wasn't anything like the weak and bullying man he had described as being his father.

Ethan was confident, yes, and occasionally arrogant, but never a bully. Neither had Mia ever known him to drink anything but the occasional glass of wine socially. And she had never seen him out of control when he was angry. On the contrary, Ethan usually became calmer, more reasoning, when he was angry.

Any more than Mia was anything like her social butterfly of a mother, who had appeared to have no interests other than going to the beauty salon, shopping, going to her tennis club three times a week, and partying with friends…

Not that Mia had ever attributed any blame to her mother for being that way. All the Burton homes had been run very efficiently by an army of servants, Mia had been out at school all day, and William had often worked late—necessitating Kay making a social life for herself.

That social life had come to an abrupt halt after Kay's accident, resulting in her moods becoming mercurial, at best—to the point that William had decided it would be better for Mia if she went away to boarding school to attend sixth form. The school at which Grace Black had been headmistress...

Mia couldn't quite meet Ethan's gaze now. 'I liked your mother when I attended Southlands. And I'd never say she didn't have a perfect right to find happiness after she was widowed.'

'Just not with your father!'

Mia's chin tilted defensively. 'Not in the way the two of them got together, no.'

'And what way would that be, Mia?'

She moved restlessly under Ethan's narrowed gaze. 'Look, I've never thought my parents had the perfect marriage—'

'Is there such a thing?' Ethan asked dryly. 'From what I've seen, most people would consider themselves lucky if they had ten per cent of perfection in their marriage.'

'That's extremely cynical of you...'

'This coming from the woman who can't even bear to talk about her father's second wife without a sneer in her voice?'

Her father's second wife...

Chicken or the egg...?

Ethan maintained that his mother and William hadn't even met each other until Mia started attending Southlands School, and Mia was just as insistent that

William had chosen that particular school because of his relationship with Grace Black.

What if, after all this time, Mia discovered she had been wrong...?

Although, either way, William and Grace had still been a couple long before William's wife had died.

She shook her head. 'We're straying from the point, Ethan.'

'That's probably because I'm not sure what the point is any more! You're right—your parents' marriage was far from perfect, Mia. In fact—' He broke off abruptly.

'Yes?' Mia looked at him warily.

'Never mind,' Ethan muttered impatiently as he turned away. 'The point I was trying to make earlier was that, whatever your parents did or didn't feel for each other, your father has always loved you. William has photographs of you everywhere, Mia,' he continued. 'The house here in London, the villa in the South of France, the apartment in New York, the estate in Antigua. Everywhere!'

She grimaced, not happy with Ethan's 'never mind' in answer to her question about her parents, but knowing him well enough to realise from his closed expression that if Ethan knew any more on the subject he wasn't going to share it with her.

'That must be unpleasant for you!'

He gave her a reproving glance. 'My point being that William wouldn't bother doing that if looking at those photographs reminded him of something or someone unpleasant.'

Ethan made a convincing argument, Mia allowed reluctantly. Convincing enough for her to agree to go to the South of France later this afternoon after all...?

She had baked enough cookies over the weekend

Send For
2 FREE BOOKS
Today!

I accept your offer!

Please send me two
free Harlequin Presents® novels and two mystery gifts (gifts worth about $10). I understand that these books are completely free—even the shipping and handling will be paid—and I am under no obligation to purchase anything, ever, as explained on the back of this card.

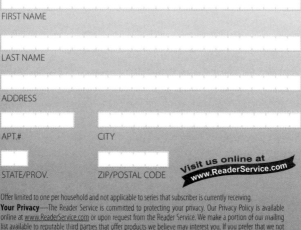

❏ I prefer the regular-print edition
106/306 HDL FJEQ

❏ I prefer the larger-print edition
176/376 HDL FJEQ

Please Print

FIRST NAME

LAST NAME

ADDRESS

APT.#   CITY

STATE/PROV.   ZIP/POSTAL CODE

Visit us online at
www.ReaderService.com

to last the whole week, the coffee shop was closed all day today, and she had no doubts Dee and Matt could manage without her for a couple of days...

'Okay, Ethan.' She sighed. 'Make the arrangements for me to fly over this afternoon. But I can't stay long—'

'Let's not start out by putting time limits on this before you've even left England.' Ethan deliberately kept his tone light, revealing none of the inner satisfaction he was feeling at Mia's capitulation.

Mia looked less certain of herself now. 'How will you—? How do you intend letting my father know of my arrival...?'

'My mother, of course.'

'Of course.'

Ethan's mouth tightened at the heaviness of Mia's tone. 'If you can think of some other way of breaking the news to William without his having another heart attack I'd be glad to hear it.'

Mia seemed to give the question thought for several long seconds, before giving a defeated sigh. 'I can't.'

'Cheer up, Mia,' he drawled mockingly. 'Think of this as being your good deed for the decade!'

Her eyes flashed. 'You really don't have a very good opinion of me, do you...?'

He shrugged. 'I'm reserving judgement.'

'You didn't seem too bothered as to whether or not you liked me on Friday evening!'

Ethan wasn't bothered by it now, either. How could he be when just being in the same room with Mia again was enough to make him so physically aware of her? Ethan wanted to strip her out of that businesslike black suit and pale green blouse before lying her across his desk and devouring her.

A move no doubt guaranteed to ensure that Mia

changed her mind about going to the South of France
or anywhere else later today…

'Perhaps.' He nodded abruptly before moving to sit
back behind his desk. 'I'll give you a call later this morning to let you know what time I've arranged the flight
for, and when I'll be picking you up and driving to the
private airfield.'

Mia frowned. 'I'm quite capable of getting a taxi if
you tell me where I need to go.'

'I don't think you've quite understood me, Mia.' Ethan
gave an amused smile. 'I'm coming with you to the South
of France.'

Mia's eyes widened in alarm. 'I'm not a child that
needs you to take me anywhere!'

'I'm well aware of the fact that you aren't a child,
Mia,' he acknowledged wearily. 'I just think it would
be…better for all concerned if I came along too.'

No doubt Ethan's presence would make this 'better'
for William—and for Grace, Mia accepted. But would
his being there make it any easier for *her*?

Much as she found being in Ethan's company disturbing, in this particular situation she believed she might
also find it somehow reassuring. 'Okay, Ethan, we'll do
this your way,' Mia conceded heavily. 'But don't expect
there to be any happy-ever-after ending to this meeting, because it just isn't going to happen,' she said with
certainty.

'We'll see,' he murmured softly. 'And Mia…?' He
stopped her as she turned away to walk briskly over to
the door.

Mia turned slowly, remembering the last time they
had parted like this—and the resultant mess she'd had to
clear up after smashing the wine glass against the door!
'Yes…?'

Ethan gave a mocking smile, as if he too were remembering hearing glass shatter against wood as he left her apartment on Friday evening. 'Remember to pack your bikini; it may be cold here, but it's still warm in the South of France!'

Pack her bikini? As if! 'I'm only doing this to set my father's mind at rest concerning my wellbeing, Ethan— not going on holiday!'

'Pity,' he said softly, that lazy grey gaze moving over her slowly, knowingly, from her the top of her golden head to her stiletto-shoe toes.

Reminding Mia all too forcibly of the fact that Ethan had seen at least half of her completely naked on Friday evening… That he had kissed her with those sensually sculptured lips, and those elegant hands now resting on his desktop had caressed every inch of her…

She drew in a ragged breath. 'I'll see you later this afternoon.'

'Count on it,' he confirmed.

It took every ounce of Mia's rapidly wavering self-confidence to continue walking to the door, all the time totally aware of him watching her every step of the way…

CHAPTER EIGHT

'COMFORTABLE?'

Who wouldn't be comfortable in this luxurious private jet, with its plush carpet, extensive bar and kitchen area, eight fixed easy chairs arranged about two coffee tables, and your own personal cabin stewardess to welcome your aboard and see to your every need?

Mia had travelled extensively with her parents when she was a child, and they had always travelled first class, but this private jet was something else completely…

'Business must be good,' she stated dryly, and avoided looking at Ethan sitting opposite her by concentrating on securing her seat belt instead.

Having telephoned her earlier, as he had said he would, Ethan had duly arrived at the coffee shop at three-thirty in order to drive them both to a private airstrip. A beautiful blonde stewardess had greeted them as they'd come on board, and the pilot had come through to say hello too, before returning to the cockpit to prepare for take-off.

'It is,' Ethan confirmed.

Mia gave their surroundings another brief glance rather than look directly at the ruggedly disturbing Ethan. He was casually dressed this afternoon, in jeans and a dark grey polo shirt beneath a black leather jacket, his dark hair slightly windswept from leaving the car to board the plane. Mia had been nerve-janglingly aware of everything about him since the moment she'd come down the stairs from her apartment and opened the door to him...

'Is that the bathroom through there?' She nodded in the direction of the closed door at the opposite end of the plane from the cockpit.

'And a bedroom.'

Mia turned back sharply to look at him, colour warming her cheeks as she saw the open mockery in Ethan's expression. She remembered his earlier comment concerning 'somewhere with the luxury of a bed' when he collected on his debt!

'A bedroom...?'

He shrugged broad shoulders. 'It's so that William can rest comfortably on long flights.'

'Really?' She glanced down the cabin to where Karen, the perky blonde stewardess, stood behind the bar, busily preparing the drinks they had requested. 'No doubt *you* find it "comfortable" for use during long flights, too?'

There was absolutely no way that Ethan could misunderstand Mia's implication. Or his own disinclination to satisfy that curiosity.

He had almost made a serious error in his office earlier, when his inappropriate arousal and Mia's coolness had almost goaded him into revealing the unhappy state of Mia's parents' marriage .

He was determined not to allow Mia to get under his skin to that extent again. 'For future reference, Karen happens to be married to the pilot.'

'Oh.' Mia had the grace to look embarrassed. 'That's—convenient.'

'And if you want a list of the women I've slept with

during the past five years then I suggest you come right out and ask, rather than make random insinuations,' he added.

She bristled. 'I have absolutely *no* interest in knowing who you've slept with during the past five years!'

'No?' Ethan mocked.

'No.'

'Not even a little bit interested?'

'No!'

Ethan gave a lazily satisfied smile as Mia's obvious agitation indicated the opposite. He really did like her hair in that shorter style, in fact his fingers itched to become entangled in it as he took her in his arms and—

'Can I get you anything else before take-off, Mr Black, Miss Burton?' A smiling Karen delivered their drinks to the table—sparkling water for Ethan and an orange juice for Mia.

'Not for me, thank you,' Mia refused warmly.

'We're fine, thanks.' Ethan gave the other woman a light smile, that smile fading as he leant forward across the coffee table. 'Whereas I would be very interested to hear how many men you have slept with the past five years…'

Mia was about to take a sip of her orange juice, but instead of sipping she drew in a startled breath, resulting in the juice going up her nose rather than down her throat. She instantly began to choke, inelegantly snorting juice out of her nose as she coughed and spluttered and her eyes began to stream with pained tears.

'Here.' Ethan stood up and went down on his haunches beside Mia as he handed her one of the small cloth napkins Karen had brought with their drinks. 'Looks like you're going to need to change out of that damp jumper and denims after take-off...' he murmured unapologetically.

'I'm sure that won't be necessary.' Mia shot him a belligerent glance as she began to mop up the sticky juice from the front of the cream sweater and black denims she had worn to travel in. 'I have some clean clothes in my bag I can change into before we land,' she said as the roar of the jet's engines warned that take-off was imminent.

'Is everything okay, Mr Black?' A concerned Karen had appeared beside them.

'Miss Burton just had a small accident with her juice,' Ethan dismissed as he straightened.

As if the spill had been Mia's own fault! When in fact it had been Ethan—with his far from impersonal remark about Mia's private life—who had caused her to choke and splutter.

'I'm fine.' She looked up to smile at the other woman as she handed her the damp napkin, waiting until Karen had returned to her seat at the front of the plane before turning to glare at Ethan as he resumed his own seat. 'For your future reference—my sex-life is absolutely none of your business!' she hissed in answer to the question that had caused all the upset.

He steadily returned her glaring gaze. 'At least I was honest about my interest.'

Yes, he had been. Too much so as far as Mia was concerned. Besides which, she had no intention of Ethan knowing that her sex-life had been non-existent the last five years. That Friday evening was the first time she had been in the least intimate with a man since she and Ethan had last made love five years ago.

It wasn't for lack of opportunity. Mia must have been invited out by at least a couple of dozen men during the last five years, and she had accepted at least half of those invitations. For an initial date, at least. None of those men had made it to a second date, let alone been invited to share Mia's bed for the night.

Because, as Mia had realised last week when she saw him again, none of those men had been Ethan…

Which was pretty pathetic of her, when Ethan had no doubt gone to bed with dozens of other women since the two of them had been together!

Her mouth firmed. 'Try being less honest!'

He gave a rueful smile. 'I thought honesty was what a woman wanted in her man?'

'Not that degree of honesty.' Mia frowned her irritation. 'And you aren't my man!'

Ethan gave a shrug. 'Maybe if you were to ask nicely…?'

Mia's heart gave a lurch as the jet taxied down the runway before taking off smoothly. 'If you're trying to distract my attention from the fact that I'm on my way to see my father for the first time in five years, then don't bother!' She eyed Ethan scathingly.

Was that what Ethan had been doing? In truth, he wasn't really sure *what* he had been doing. Hadn't really been sure since seeing Mia again on Thursday. Which was quite an admission from a man who always made a point of knowing exactly what he was doing, and why!

'You would rather I just left you to wallow in your own self-pity for a couple of hours?' he came back challengingly.

Her eyes widened. 'I'm not feeling in the least self-pitying.'

Ethan studied her intently. 'Then what are you feeling…?'

What *was* Mia feeling?

In regard to Ethan—too damned aware of him for her own peace of mind!

In regard to seeing her father again…? Tense? Apprehensive? Maybe even a little scared…?

Mia had always been something of a 'Daddy's girl'— even more so after her mother's accident had brought them closer still—and although Ethan probably wouldn't believe her she had deeply missed that closeness with her father after walking out five years ago. The thought of seeing him again, of the two of them perhaps being strangers to each other, was enough to tie Mia's stomach up in knots.

As for seeing Grace again…

'Nervous,' Mia admitted abruptly.

Ethan's expression softened slightly. 'If it's any consolation I believe William, after the obvious initial elation at knowing you're alive and well, is feeling just as apprehensive about meeting you again, too.'

Was it a consolation? In a way it was, yes, Mia realized, as some of the tension began to ease from the stiffness of her shoulders. 'Your mother has already spoken to him?'

Ethan gave a slight inclination of his head. 'Not the easiest conversation she's ever undertaken, I gather.'

No, Mia could imagine that it wouldn't have been. In fact she had no idea how Grace would even have gone about starting such a conversation.

'Talking of my mother…'

Mia's gaze was wary as it met Ethan's narrowed one across the width of the coffee table. 'Yes?'

'I would advise that you keep your opinions to yourself where she's concerned.'

Her brows rose. 'Threats, Ethan?'

'Not at all,' he said easily. 'I'm sure my mother is

perfectly capable of dealing with any amount of rudeness shown to her—from you or anyone else.' There was a wealth of admiration in his voice. 'My warning was in regard to William; I very much doubt he would take kindly to any slight you might try to give Grace,' he added ruefully.

Mia's mouth firmed. 'I'm well aware of where my father's loyalties now lie!'

Ethan sighed his frustration. 'It's never been a question of loyalties—'

'Could we just stop talking now, Ethan?' Mia sighed. 'I'm irritable and tired and would prefer to take a nap rather than talk any more.'

'Like me to show you where the bedroom is...?'

'I already know exactly where the bedroom is, and I'm perfectly happy napping here in the chair, thank you very much!' Her cheeks felt hot.

'Please yourself.' Ethan gave an uninterested shrug before turning away to look out of the window.

Giving Mia the opportunity to study him unobserved. Ethan looked just as arrogantly male-model gorgeous as usual, but the lines beside his eyes and mouth were deeper today, and seemed to indicate that his mood wasn't as confidently relaxed as he wished it to appear.

That perhaps he was feeling just as apprehensive about the coming meeting between Mia and her father as she was...?

'Stop fussing, Mia, you look fine!'

Easy for Ethan to say, Mia fretted inwardly as she sat beside him. He was behind the wheel of the car that had been waiting for them at the private airstrip. As she had said she would, Mia had changed out of her stained sweater and jeans into a fitted green sweater and short denim skirt before leaving the plane, and—as Ethan had just pointed out so impatiently!—she had started fidgeting more with the hem of that skirt the closer they got to her father's villa.

It was just after nine o'clock in the evening. The traffic had been heavy on the motorways, less so after they turned off towards Grasse, and almost non-existent now as they drove up the narrow roads into the hills above the town.

At any other time, and with any other reason, Mia would have enjoyed being back amongst these fragrant and beautiful terraced hills; in the past she had always loved spending the summer months here. But knowing they were only a mile or so from the villa now, from seeing her father again, made Mia feel far too apprehensive to be able to appreciate the warmth of the darkening evening and the ever-present sound of the bullfrogs croaking.

She turned to look at Ethan. 'I didn't think to ask earlier... Is leaving England so suddenly inconveniencing you in any way?'

He gave her a brief glance. 'Professionally or socially?'

Mia's mouth thinned. 'Professionally, of course.'

'Of course,' he echoed. 'Is this a trick question? If I say no, then you'll obviously assume I don't have enough to occupy my time as CEO of Burton Industries. And if I say yes, you'll then say good?'

Mia gave a pained frown. 'I don't think I have ever given you reason to call me spiteful, Ethan...'

No, she hadn't, Ethan conceded. He still wasn't completely sure of the Mia who sat beside him now, but since being with her again—talking with her, hearing the reasons she had disappeared five years ago—he certainly didn't think that had been done out of spite, but rather a sense of self-preservation. Her mother's suicide and the knowledge of her father's relationship with Grace all coming at the same time had just been too much for Mia to deal with. Their own relationship had just become a part of that whole emotional mess she had wanted to escape from...

'Sorry.' Ethan gave a brief apologetic smile even as he continued to keep his gaze on the narrow and winding road ahead. 'And, no, it wasn't too difficult to cancel my appointments for the next couple of days.'

'I'm glad— Oh, good Lord...!' Mia gave a low groan as the lights of her father's villa came into view. All of them. The place was lit up like the proverbial Christmas tree! In expectation of their arrival? Probably, Mia acknowledged warily...

Ethan gave her another quick glance. 'It really is going to be okay, Mia.'

'I'm just not sure I can do this!' Her heart was now thumping so loudly in her chest that she was sure Ethan must be able to hear it too. Her hands tightly gripped the seat either side of her, her nails digging into the soft leather.

Ethan parked the car in front of the huge closed electronically operated iron gates at the entrance of the driveway, lowering the window but making no effort to press the intercom and ask for admittance. Instead he turned in his seat to look Mia. She looked very young in the moonlight, her face white, her eyes dark and apprehensive as she looked back at him.

'Come here.' Ethan reached out and took Mia in his arms, instantly becoming aware of how much she was trembling. 'It's going to be fine, Mia,' he murmured soothingly, even as her head rested against his shoulder and her hands clung to the front of his polo shirt. '*You're* going to be fine,' he added firmly. 'The only thing you have to remember—the only thing that really matters—is that William loves you.'

Mia pulled away slightly, her eyes glittering with unshed tears as she looked up at him in the darkness. 'But what if when I see him again I realise that I no longer love him?'

'Of *course* you love him!' Ethan frowned down at her. 'He's the same man who sat on your bed and read you bedtime stories when you were very young. Who put you up on the back of a horse for the first time when you were five. Who taught you to ride a bicycle when you were six. Who—'

'How do you know those things, Ethan?' Mia breathed as she looked up at him incredulously.

He quirked one dark brow. 'How do you think I know…?'

'My father…'

'Of course.' Ethan smiled down at her. 'You obviously have no idea how proud he's always been—still is—of his only daughter! He's going to be even more impressed once he hears of the financial success you've made of Coffee and Cookies.'

Mia blinked up at him. 'You think…?'

'I am, so I know he's going to be, too.'

Mia gave him a startled glance. Ethan was impressed by her success with Coffee and Cookies…? 'It's just a coffee shop—'

'It's *your* coffee shop, and you've made it uniquely your own,' he added admiringly. 'The couple of dozen boxes of cookies you sell every week to several specialist shops in town don't do the coffee shop's reputation, or your own, any harm either!'

Strangely, at the last moment Mia had decided to pack one of those boxes of cookies in her small overnight suitcase.

She had told herself it was so she had something to snack on if she needed to, but could the real reason have been because deep down she had wanted to show her father that she had made a success of her life this past five years? Nowhere near the scope of the worldwide successes of Burton Industries, of course, but nevertheless Mia was proud of what she had managed to achieve by the sweat of her own brow.

'I've sampled the product, remember?' Ethan continued dryly. 'I have no idea what your recipe is, but your cookies are orgasmically good!'

Mia's cheeks suddenly felt warm as she clearly remembered Ethan's groans of pleasure as he ate one of her triple chocolate cookies. So similar to the groans of pleasure he made during lovemaking...

'Is this another effort on your part to distract me?' she murmured, so very aware now that Ethan still held her in his arms, and that his chest felt very warm against her breasts through the thin wool of her sweater.

Ethan's eyes glittered silver as he looked down at her. 'Is it working?'

Mia was held captive by that mercurial gaze, her mouth feeling suddenly dry. 'Oh, yes...'

'Good,' Ethan said softly, his gaze moving down to the lure of Mia's slightly parted lips. Full and sensuous lips that he knew would feel soft and warm beneath his—that *were* soft and warm as he gave in to that temptation and lowered his head to capture them with his own!

He had been wanting to do this again since—hell, since Friday evening!

Ethan had spent the whole time Mia had been asleep on the plane watching her unobserved. Lingering the longest on the fullness of her lips above that firm and determined chin...

Lips that he now parted with a single sweep of his tongue, pulling Mia more firmly into his arms and crushing her breasts against his chest as he curved her into him before deepening the kiss. Mia's fingers became entangled in the dark thickness of Ethan's hair as she returned the heat of those kisses, the ragged sound of their breathing blocking out even the noisy croaking of the bullfrogs.

Ethan's arousal was instantaneous, together with the need he felt to lay Mia down across the seat and dispense with the barrier of their clothes...

'Ethan? Ethan, is that you?'

It took Mia several precious seconds, and several greedy kisses, to realise that the voice she could hear was real and not a figment of her overheated senses. For her to recognise the disembodied voice coming over the intercom outside the window as belonging to Grace.

That recognition had the same dampening effect on Mia as having a bucket of ice-cold water thrown over her!

CHAPTER NINE

'DO YOU think you could try looking a little less as if you're paying a visit to the dentist?' Ethan rasped his impatience—and his sexual frustration!—as the two of them got out of the car parked in front of the brightly lit villa.

Not that he could exactly blame Mia for putting such an abrupt end to those passionate kisses—Ethan had found it more than a little deflating to his own libido to hear the sound of his mother's voice when his thoughts, his emotions, were so deeply enmeshed with stripping Mia naked!

Even so, Mia could have looked at him with a little less revulsion as she pulled sharply out of his arms and moved as far back in her seat as it was possible for her to go.

Giving Ethan the impression that he had turned into some sort of monster she should avoid even coming into contact with! Or, perhaps more accurately, as if that voice had just reminded Mia that he was Grace Black's son...

His jaw tightened. 'Shall we just get this over and done with?'

Mia's face was pale once again, her green eyes huge in that pallor as she looked over at him. 'I have no idea what I'm supposed to say when I see my father again, let alone your mother!'

'I'm sure you'll think of something.' Ethan gave an uninterested shrug before moving to the back of the car to take their two small cases out of the boot.

Mia wasn't so sure... She hadn't seen her father for five years,

Grace for even longer than that; exactly what *did* you say to a father in these circumstances, or to the woman he had married within months of the death of your own mother?

Ethan seemed to feel no such reluctance as he strode past her with their suitcases and began to ascend the stone steps leading up to the front of the villa. As if those passionately heated kisses of a few minutes ago had no significance whatsoever, Mia accepted heavily as she slowly followed him up the steps.

And maybe to Ethan they hadn't? He had been intent on distracting Mia since picking her up from her apartment earlier this afternoon, in any way available to him. It would be ridiculous of Mia to hope those kisses had meant anything to him other than adding to that distraction.

Even if they had meant much more than that to her...

Much as Mia might try to deny it, to distance herself, her physical response to Ethan burned just as strongly as it ever had. Perhaps, with maturity, even more so.

Mia's meandering thoughts came to an abrupt halt, and so did she, as the front door of the villa was thrown open, light spilling out around them as her father stood silhouetted in the doorway.

Mia's breath caught in her throat, and her heart stopped beating in her chest as she looked up at him and instantly saw both how little, and yet how much, he had changed in the last five years. He was thinner than he used to be, and at the same time still as tall and strong. His iron-grey hair showed signs of having turned white at his temples. His face was as ruggedly handsome, and yet it too was thinner, with more lines beside his eyes and mouth than Mia remembered being there.

That sense of numbed disorientation seemed to last for hours, and yet Mia knew it had only been seconds as this new image of William became superimposed on the old one, so that he was suddenly just her father. Strong. Handsome. The rock Mia had always been able to depend upon.

Mia's eyes misted over with tears as she saw the hungry pleasure that lit up her father's eyes as he gazed his fill of her. She took a step towards him, only to come to an abrupt halt as she saw movement in the tiled hallway behind William, along with a brief flash of auburn hair. Instantly she recognised the elegantly lovely Grace as she hovered there supportively.

As if she might rush forward and catch William if he should fall.

Or as if she might step into the breach should Mia say or do anything to upset him…

Mia tensed as her gaze returned to her father. 'You're looking well.' Her tone was stilted.

That glow of pleasure in his eyes flickered and then died, and there was the briefest slump of his shoulders before he straightened determinedly. 'And you've cut off your beautiful hair,' he murmured lightly.

Was that a good thing or a bad thing? Did she look more like her glamorous mother or less so?

Mia raised a self-conscious hand to those feathered wisps of gold.

'I find it easier to deal with when I'm getting ready for work in the morning.'

Her father nodded briefly. 'Ethan told us that you run a very successful coffee shop in London.'

Mia had been concentrating so hard on her father that she had briefly blocked out the fact that Ethan was there too, but she glanced at him now as he moved forward to place their suitcases in the hall, before greeting his mother and so giving Mia her first real look at the woman who was now married to her father.

Grace Black the headmistress had always possessed a calm and likeable elegance, but Grace Burton had an added relaxed contentment to her lovely features. Those beautiful blue eyes were now glowing with pride as she hugged her son, the arms the two of them kept about each other's waist as they stepped out onto the terrace evidence of the closeness of their relationship.

And at the same time seeming only to emphasise the awkwardness that now existed between Mia and her father...

Ethan frowned as he looked across at father and daughter. He had known this was going to be difficult— he just hadn't appreciated how difficult. Mia was so tense and defensive, and William's initial pleasure had turned to obvious disappointment as Mia kept her distance from him.

'Shall we all go inside?' he suggested lightly. 'I'm sure Mia is as much in need of a hot drink as I am!'

Mia shot him a grateful glance. 'Tea would be good,' she acknowledged quietly.

'Of course.' William seemed to drag himself out of whatever memories he had been lost in as he stood back to allow Mia to enter the villa ahead of him.

Ethan frowned again as Mia stepped fully into the

light and he saw just how pale she was. The expression in her eyes was one of dazed bewilderment. His earlier irritation with her dissipated as he accepted that only hours ago Mia had still been in England, safe in the certainty of the life she had made for herself there. Now, only hours later, she had been thrust right back into the same maelstrom of emotions—and the same people— she had felt she so desperately needed to escape from five years ago.

'Mia,' Ethan's mother murmured softly as the two women came face to face for the first time.

'Mrs—Grace.' Mia nodded abruptly before stepping into the hallway and disappearing inside the villa, obviously no longer sure how to address her previous headmistress.

Mia had warned Ethan not to expect any happy-ever-after ending to this meeting with her father, but he really hadn't expected it to be quite as strained as it so obviously was. Naive of him, perhaps, but a part of Ethan had always thought—hoped?—that once Mia saw William again everything else would just fall into place.

'Give her time,' his mother said with an encouraging squeeze of his arm.

'She's already had five years, damn it,' he growled, only too aware that he was responsible for bringing about this meeting. A meeting that could still blow up in their faces...

'Then it isn't going to hurt to give her a little longer, is it?' Grace moved away to tuck her hand into the crook of William's arm, her smile warmly comforting as the two of them talked quietly together.

Ethan gave them a last concerned glance before following Mia inside. She stood in the hallway, obviously not comfortable with the idea of just walking into the sitting room as she would once have done.

Ethan gave a frustrated sigh. 'You—'

'If you're going to start yelling at me—don't!' Mia's voice broke emotionally, her eyes awash with unshed tears.

His expression instantly softened. 'I never yell, Mia.'

No, he didn't, Mia acknowledged ruefully; another legacy of that bullying and inebriate father, perhaps? Whatever the reason, Ethan had never felt the need to so much as raise his voice in her company, or anyone else's, in order to convey his displeasure over something.

Her throat felt uncomfortably dry as she swallowed before speaking. 'I warned you I wouldn't know what to say or do when I saw my father again!' She gave a glance to where her father and Grace were still in muted conversation together on the terrace.

'You did just fine,' Ethan said, before he too glanced at the other couple. 'I would imagine my mother is offering William the same reassurances!' he added dryly.

Mia paused as she saw the way the older couple stood so comfortably together. 'They're happy together, aren't they...?'

'Very.'

She nodded. 'You shouldn't have brought me here, Ethan.'

'Because?'

'Because I don't belong here.'

'And why is that?' he prompted.

Ethan knew why! Knew that Mia had only needed to see her father and Grace together to know that she wasn't really apart of this scenario. For her to also realise her parents had never seemed this—this relaxed and comfortable in each other's company...

Mia had always considered that her childhood—with a workaholic father and a socially busy mother—was no different from any of her friends'. That everyone's mother was out at the theatre, or attending dinner parties or being hostess at one, every evening of the week. That everyone's father was so busy working that it often precluded him joining his wife and children when they went away during the school holidays, as Mia and Kay had always done, going to stay at one of their many other homes around the world—somewhere hot in the summer and the ski lodge in Aspen during the winter. William had usually managed to join them for a few days, and they would be busy days, spent by the pool or on the ski slopes, before they all met up with her mother's friends for dinner at one of the fashionable restaurants she favoured.

All that had changed after her mother's car accident, of course, but during those early years it had all seemed so perfect to the child Mia had been.

Remembering that now, looking through the eyes of an adult at the weeks, months, her parents had often spent apart, Mia couldn't help but wonder if it really had been as idyllic as she had always thought it was, or if Ethan's description this morning of her parents' marriage being 'far from perfect' wasn't a more accurate one.

'If you would like to go through to the sitting room I'll go and make us all some tea?' Grace Burton prompted lightly as she and William came back inside the villa.

'Perhaps Mia would like to come and help?' Ethan answered his mother, but it was Mia he looked at as he spoke, dark brows raised in challenge.

She shot him a glowering glance before frowning across at Grace. 'Doesn't Marie work here any more...?' The plump and bustling Frenchwoman had been caretaker of the villa when the Burtons weren't in residence, falling into the role of housekeeper when they were. She would probably be in her mid-fifties by now, but even so...

'She retired two years ago,' the older woman replied smoothly.

No doubt only the first of many changes Grace had made since becoming mistress of the Burton households!

'Marie has a young disabled granddaughter she wanted to spend more time with.' Mia's father was the one to explain firmly, as he obviously sensed her unspoken criticism. 'Grace prefers to do our little bit of cooking herself, anyway.' He looked at his wife admiringly. 'So we just have a young girl from the village come in a couple of times a week now, to do the heavier cleaning.'

A brief glance at her father's face showed Mia that his expression was as disapproving as his tone as he looked at her, before his features relaxed as he turned to look at Grace. 'I'm quite happy to help make the tea.' Mia shrugged.

'Did you bring along some of your cookies to go with it...?' Ethan questioned.

'No, I didn't,' Mia denied sharply—and then just as quickly felt guilty colour wash over her cheeks as she instantly thought of the box of assorted cookies sitting on top of her clothes in the small suitcase.

Ethan gave her a knowing look. 'Pity...'

'I'm really interested to hear about this coffee shop of yours, Mia,' her father put in enthusiastically.

She gave an awkward shrug. 'It's just like a dozen others in any busy high street.'

'Rubbish,' Ethan dismissed impatiently. 'The place is

always packed with people, and I can personally vouch for the fact that Mia's triple chocolate cookies are—'

'Popular,' Mia put in quickly, in an effort to stop Ethan from repeating his earlier risqué comment.

'Unlike anything else I've ever tasted,' Ethan finished dryly.

'Let's go and make that tea, Mia.' Grace suggested firmly, at the same time as she gave her son a questioning glance at that other conversation she sensed beneath his casual remarks.

Being alone with the other woman was the last thing Mia wanted, but without making a scene immediately on her arrival she really had to go along with the suggestion. Besides which, the other woman's headmistress-like tone was such that Mia didn't feel she had any other choice but to trail silently after Grace as she went through to the rustic kitchen at the back of the villa!

No doubt the two men would find their own conversation flowed far more easily once the women had left than any conversation was likely to do between Grace and Mia...

'Mia seems so...different.'

Ethan gave the older man a sympathetic glance even as he inwardly wondered how Mia and his mother would get along together in the kitchen; Mia's reluctance to be alone with Grace had been more than obvious. 'Only superficially. Fundamentally she's still the same Mia,' he said, and realised that it was true; beneath all that prickly self-defence Mia was still the same warm and caring woman Ethan had known five years ago.

Dangerously so...?

Because there was more to Mia now than just warmth and caring, and her obvious beauty and intelligence. She now possessed an added self-confidence after having succeeded in her business enterprise, making her a deadly combination for any man.

Ethan frowned slightly as he thought of the way Mia had evaded answering him earlier when he had asked if she'd had other lovers. That frown deepened as he acknowledged he didn't like the thought of any other men in her life this past five years.

He had discovered on their first night together that he was Mia's first lover, and had tempered his lovemaking accordingly as he gently introduced her to the delights of such intimacy. He had never been any woman's first lover before, and although Mia probably didn't realise it—and wouldn't care even if she did!—Ethan had always valued the fact that he had been her first lover. If not her last.

Which was probably *not* something he should be thinking about while talking to Mia's father!

He gave William a rueful smile. 'I believe she feels just as awkward about this meeting as you do.'

William gave a sad shake of his head. 'She's still angry with me.'

'Not as much as she thinks she is,' Ethan said slowly, having seen the hunger in Mia's eyes as she had looked up and seen her father again for the first time in five years, even if she hadn't been aware of it herself.

'I hope you're right.' The older man suddenly looked worried. 'Perhaps we shouldn't have let the two women go off alone together just yet…? I wouldn't want Mia to say anything that might upset Grace.'

Ethan smiled more confidently. 'My mother is perfectly capable of taking care of herself, I assure you.'

William looked no less concerned after his assurances. 'I hope you're right…'

* * *

'So, Mia, how have you really been?' Grace moved efficiently about the rustic terracotta kitchen as she prepared the tea things.

In fact the other woman moved about the kitchen so confidently that Mia felt slightly superfluous. Especially so as Grace's quiet efficiency alerted her to the fact that her own mother had probably never even stepped inside this kitchen, let alone made tea for herself or the family.

Kay had never particularly liked the villa William had bought 'in the wilds of nowhere' in the South of France, and would much rather it had been in one of the more fashionable resorts along the coast, where all of her friends had had villas or apartments. As such, Kay had come here as little as possible, and even when she had as often as not she'd left Mia and William beside the pool for the day while she went off shopping, or to Monte Carlo with friends.

More memories from her childhood came as Mia stood in front of the kitchen window, looking out over the familiar valley. The lights of several other villas were shining in the darkness, and the brighter lights of Cannes glowed in the distance.

She turned now to look at Grace with guarded eyes. 'I've been very well. You?' she prompted stiltedly.

Grace shrugged. 'The scare we had with William six months ago was…cause for concern, of course, but he seems to have recovered very well.'

There was no rebuke in the other woman's tone, and yet Mia still felt guilty at the part she had played— albeit innocently—in her father's heart attack. 'Ethan told me.'

'Did he…?'

'Well, he showed me those photographs my father

somehow…acquired.' Mia grimaced as she recalled the awful images.

Grace looked concerned. 'He shouldn't have done that.'

'Drastic measures…' Mia gave a shrug, knowing she probably wouldn't be here now if Ethan hadn't shown her those photographs. 'I really had no idea my father would still be looking for me after all this time.'

Grace gave her a pained glance. 'He's never stopped looking for you, Mia.'

Mia bristled defensively. 'I left him a note telling him not to.'

Grace gave a sad smile. 'William still has that note. He carries it about with him in his wallet. Along with the last photograph of the two of you together.'

Mia drew in a pained breath. 'I never meant to hurt him—'

'And yet you did.'

Her cheeks warmed at the gentle rebuke. 'As I said, I never meant to. Look, Grace.' She rallied determinedly. 'I appreciate my having come here is difficult for my father, for Ethan, and most especially for you—'

'Most especially for me?' Grace looked at her quizzically. 'Why on earth should *I* find your being here in the least difficult? You're William's daughter, as Ethan is my son, and there has never been a problem with Ethan visiting us.'

'It's not the same…' She gave a shake of her head.

'You're wrong there, Mia. It's exactly the same. The cups are still in the same cupboard as they always were, if you would like to get them for me?' Grace prompted as she began to place milk and sugar on the tray.

Mia moved automatically to the correct cupboard and

took out four cups and saucers before handing them to the older woman. 'I'll only be staying a day or so—'

'Why?' Grace pierced her with those candid blue eyes.

She shrugged. 'For one thing, I have a business to run.'

'And for another...?'

Mia sighed her impatience. 'I'm sure that Ethan has explained to you that I've only come here at all in order to reassure my father that there will be no more photographs of—of dead bodies found in ditches for him to look at and imagine they might be me!'

'He has, yes,' the older woman murmured. 'And you don't think that reassurance might take a little more time than a day or so...?'

Her mouth firmed. 'No.'

Grace nodded without further comment. 'What about Ethan?'

Mia frowned. 'What about him?'

'Exactly.'

'I'm sorry?' Mia gave a puzzled shake of her head. 'I have no idea what you're talking about.'

Grace looked at her speculatively. 'You know, Mia, you were one of my brightest pupils. Intelligent and studious, you left Southlands School with four first-class A levels.'

Mia had lost this conversation somewhere. 'You think perhaps I should have done something more with those A levels than open a coffee shop—'

'Not at all,' the other woman dismissed. 'I always knew that you would succeed at whatever you chose to do with your life, and from the little Ethan has told us that's exactly what your coffee shop appears to be—a success. It's only in the emotional side of your life that you appear to be somewhat…lacking in insight.'

Yes, Grace had definitely lost her. Unless… 'If you're attempting to criticise my mother because she was something of a social lightweight rather than an academic like you—'

'I wouldn't dream of criticising your mother, Mia. In any way.' Grace sounded shocked at the suggestion, and every inch Mia's previous headmistress.

'Then I don't understand…'

'My reference was to your past relationship with Ethan, of course.'

'My…?' Mia gave a dazed shake of her head, her cheeks feeling suddenly warm. 'What does that have to do with the here and now?'

'The two of you were a couple before you disappeared so suddenly,' Grace reminded her gently.

'And?'

'And have the two of you managed to resolve your own…differences at last?'

Mia's mouth tightened as she thought of the way she and Ethan were together now. 'No,' she bit out abruptly.

'Pity,' the older woman said quietly.

'I'm sure you don't mean that!'

Grace looked puzzled. 'Why wouldn't I…?'

'Because Ethan was never serious about me—was only using me in the same way that you—'

'Careful, Mia…' Grace warned.

'Or what?' she mused ruefully. 'What else can anyone do to me? I haven't even seen my own father for the past five years—'

'And whose fault is that?'

'My own,' Mia accepted heavily. 'But at the time I felt

I had no other choice but to distance myself from—from all of you.'

'And now?'

She shrugged. 'Now you're married to my father and Ethan is CEO of his company!'

'I happen to love your father.' The older woman looked at her steadily. 'As for Ethan—do you think this was all he ever wanted to do with his life?' Impatience underscored Grace's tone. 'That he never had any ambitions of his own?' She shook her head. 'Look at him, Mia—really look at my son—and then tell me if you think Ethan is truly a man whose only ambition was to run another man's company for him!'

Mia had been deeply in love with the fun-loving and passionate Ethan she had known five years ago, but she wasn't sure what to make of the Ethan he was now…

'As you've already made it clear you don't intend to stay here for long, I have nothing to lose by speaking plainly,' the older woman continued briskly.

Mia stiffened. 'No.'

Grace gave a rueful smile. 'It might be easier to do if you didn't look quite so much like William!' She gave a self-derisive shake of her head.

'Like…? You're wrong.' Mia shook her head. 'I've always looked far more like my mother than my father.'

'In your colouring, perhaps,' Grace allowed. 'But the rest of you is definitely all William. And I've never been able to stay angry with him for very long, either.' She looked at Mia searchingly. 'You genuinely have no idea what your leaving in that way five years ago did—to William, to Ethan, to this whole family—do you?'

'Maybe not, but I do know that you and Ethan should be thanking me for leaving the way clear for you both to move into my father's life rather criticising me for going!' Mia came back abruptly.

Grace gave an exasperated smile. 'I believe William should have spanked your bottom more often when you were a child.'

'He didn't spank me at all!'

'Then perhaps he should have done,' Grace murmured dryly. 'I'm truly surprised that Ethan hasn't tried to shake or kiss some sense into you this past few days, at least!'

'He's already tried doing both those things—obviously they failed!' Mia drawled dryly.

Grace eyed her speculatively. 'Interesting...'

'In what way?'

The older woman gave a brief shrug. 'Forgive me for saying so, Mia, but I was under the impression that you were in love with Ethan five years ago...'

'No, I most certainly *don't* forgive you!' Mia bristled, humiliated colour darkening her cheeks at the obvious transparency of her youthful emotion. 'And I am not that naive and trusting fool any longer!'

The older woman continued to look at her for several long seconds, before giving a sad grimace. 'You may have the men in this family jumping through emotional hoops, Mia, but I should warn you I have no intention of doing the same. Not only because I don't feel I have anything to apologise for, but also because I don't believe it's good for you,' she added chidingly. 'In other words, it really *is* time you opened your eyes to the truth that has always been right under your nose if you cared to look for it!'

CHAPTER TEN

'HAVING trouble sleeping…?'

Mia didn't know whether to be irritated or just accepting when Ethan interrupted her as she sat still and quiet in the darkness on the terrace that looked down towards the welcoming glow of Cannes on the horizon.

The conversation earlier, as the four of them sat in the comfort of the sitting room drinking tea together, had been as politely stilted as Mia had suspected it might be: the comfort of their flight over, the weather tomorrow, the possibility of having lunch at one of the local restaurants. Mia wasn't even sure she would still be here by lunchtime tomorrow!

By the time Grace had suggested they all have an early night and wake refreshed in the morning, Mia's nerves had been so strung out she had been the first to get to her feet and excuse herself. Only then to learn that she was to occupy the same bedroom she always had.

Ten minutes alone in the girlish familiarity of that bedroom, along with all its childhood memories, and Mia had known she had to get out of there. If only so that she could breathe easily again.

'Okay if I join you…?'

She looked up at Ethan. His face was in shadow, only the glittering intensity of his gaze visible in the moonlight, and the villa behind them was in complete darkness—evidence that William and Grace had at least taken advantage of the early night and were trying to sleep.

'Why not?'

Ethan folded his long length down into the seat beside hers.

'Are you okay?'

Was she okay? Seeing her father again, witnessing the warmth between him and Grace, along with all the past memories crowding in on her—no, Mia *wasn't* okay!

'Not really,' she understated.

'Give it time, Mia.' Ethan offered her the same advice his mother had given him earlier, knowing that this evening, being with William again under such awkward circumstances, had been very hard on Mia.

Hard on all of them, in fact. His mother gave the appearance of being her usual charming self, but nevertheless Ethan had sensed the tension beneath that outer calm. William, a man Ethan had always admired for his decisiveness, had seemed to be walking on eggshells every time he so much as spoke to Mia, while all the time his gaze devoured her, as if he still couldn't believe she was really here.

As for Mia...

The strain of being here, of seeing her father again, had been palpable—so much so that by the time she'd excused herself and gone upstairs to her room her face had been deathly pale, with dark and haunted shadows beneath her eyes.

Ethan had been sitting downstairs in the darkness of the sitting room, his mother and William having gone up to their own room only a few minutes after Mia, when he'd seen Mia moving quietly past the open doorway.

Seconds later the back door of the villa had softly opened and then closed again. For a few brief seconds Ethan had wondered if history was about to repeat itself, and she was leaving without telling any of them she was going, until he'd realised that she didn't have her small overnight bag with her.

Which was little comfort when his mother had informed him that Mia had said she might be leaving tomorrow...

She drew in a ragged breath. 'Ethan, I'm pleased that my father has recovered so well from his heart attack. I'm even...content to accept that he and your mother are obviously happy together.'

'Are you?' he growled sceptically.

Strangely, she was, Mia acknowledged. That brief, straight-talking conversation in the kitchen with Grace had reminded her of why she had once liked the older woman so much. It had also made her realise that the shock and resentment she had felt five years ago, when she'd first learnt of Grace's relationship with William, had been more on her mother's behalf than her own.

Just this past few hours in their company, witnessing the love that obviously flowed between William and Grace, had forced Mia to see that she had really had no idea of the dynamics of her own parents' marriage, let alone the reasons for William's relationship with Grace Black. No matter what the reasons might have been for that relationship initially, it had obviously endured.

Besides which, nothing that Mia or anyone else said, or did, was ever going to bring her mother back...

'Yes,' she answered firmly. 'Which in no way changes my plans to return to England tomorrow.'

Ethan drew in a frustrated breath. Damn it, he had been hoping for so much more from this visit than

Mia's acceptance of their parents' marriage. He had hoped—

'Your mother and I had an…interesting conversation earlier…'

Ethan instantly looked guarded. 'Oh?'

Mia looked at him searchingly for several minutes before nodding. 'She said that it was never your ambition to run another man's company for him…?'

Ethan looked at her from between narrowed lids, cursing the lack of light by which to read her expression, not knowing if she was just asking these questions out of perverse feminine curiosity or a real need to know.

He gave a hard smile. 'At which point you no doubt assured her that you knew better? That being CEO of Burton Industries was exactly what I've always wanted?'

Mia grimaced. 'I always thought so, yes…'

Ethan moved restlessly to his feet. 'Isn't it a little late in the day for you to start doubting yourself, Mia?'

It probably was…

And yet being with Ethan again made a part of Mia hunger to have been wrong about him all these years.

Her eyes had adjusted enough to the darkness now to take in how long and lean he looked, still wearing the clothes he had traveled over in—that grey polo-shirt fitting snugly over the tautness of his chest and stomach, the short sleeves revealing deeply muscled arms. And he smelt wonderful too—just a hint of lingering aftershave and lots of hot, lethally decadent male…!

Mia's mouth felt dry, and she moistened her lips with the tip of her tongue before attempting to speak. 'I don't know—is it?'

Ethan moved to stand beside the concrete balustrade, his face turned away from her, making it impossible to read his expression. 'I doubt you would believe me if I were to tell you I only ever intended to stay in the public sector for a few years, before eventually teaching Economics.'

'You wanted to *teach?*' There was no way Mia could keep the incredulity out of her voice.

'I said you wouldn't believe me...' A derisive smile curved Ethan's lips as he glanced back at her.

It wasn't so much that Mia didn't believe him, more a case of it just never having occurred to her...

But she thought about it now, remembering how often she had needed Ethan to explain things to her during that first awful year of taking Economics at university five years ago, and how he would do so in such a way that she actually understood what the university professors had often seemed to make totally incomprehensible.

But could she really see Ethan as a teacher...? His mother had not only been headmistress of Southlands School, but also an excellent teacher of Latin to the sixth-formers.

'It's in the blood, after all,' Ethan drawled as he seemed to read some of Mia's thoughts.

Yes, it was—maybe five years ago, before Ethan had begun to rise in the hierarchy of Burton Industries, before those years had made him into the forceful and powerful man he was today.

She gave a slow shake of her head. 'If you had your time over again—'

'I would make exactly the same choices,' Ethan bit out tautly, knowing that his loyalty and affection for William were such there *were* no other choices.

'I see.'

'Do you?' He looked at her searchingly.

She was beginning to, yes... 'Did my...leaving so suddenly have any effect on your decision?'

Ethan became even more guarded. 'Why do you want to know?'

'Possibly because I'm never going to start understanding any of this if people don't start giving me answers to my questions.'

'Look on the positive side—I would never have been able to afford my car on a teacher's salary!'

'Ethan—'

'Let's just leave it, hmm, Mia? It sounds as if my mother has already told you enough for one evening.'

'Maybe that's because your mother, at least, has decided to stop treating me like a child?' Mia snapped in frustration.

'Is that what you really want, Mia?' Ethan strode forcefully across the terrace to stand directly in front of her. 'For us all to stop treating you like a child? For *me* to stop...?'

'Yes!'

'Are you sure you're ready for what might happen next?'

Mia looked up at him in the darkness, knowing Ethan was talking about something completely different from her. She was so very aware of him now, and of the stillness of the night that surrounded them like a cocoon. A time out of time. Where nothing else mattered but Ethan and Mia. No past. No present. Certainly no future...

'I'm ready, Ethan...' she breathed huskily.

He gave a shake of his head. 'And tomorrow? What happens then?'

Mia fingertips over his lips cut off his next question. 'Stop talking so much, Ethan, and just kiss me!'

'Not until I'm completely sure you know exactly what you're asking.' He still held back.

At this moment in time, here and now, Mia knew exactly what she needed—what she wanted. It was all summed up in one word. Ethan.

She placed one of her hands against his chest. The increase of his heartbeat was evidence that he found her proximity as disturbing as she found his. Ethan felt very warm and solid as she held his gaze and let both her hands move up his chest and over his shoulders, allowing her fingers to become enmeshed in the dark hair at his nape as she moved up on her tiptoes to place her lips gently against his.

It was like a dam bursting. Ethan's arms moved fiercely about her as he deepened the kiss, and Mia was only too willing to return that heat, so hungry for the taste and feel of him.

Ethan kissed Mia with a fervour that quickly bordered on being out of control as he all but devoured the heady taste of her lips and mouth. He curved her body into his, pressed her breasts against his lower chest, and the heat of her thighs fitted snugly against his when his hands curled about her bottom to pull her in tight against them.

He broke the kiss only so that he could run his lips across Mia's arched throat. The softness of her skin tasted of some rich and exotic delight, and the ragged sound of her breathing was an erotic rasp, making Ethan ache with need.

'Dear God, Mia…!' Ethan breathed harshly as he raised his head to look down at the flushed beauty of her face in the moonlight, able to see the dark and hungry passion in her eyes and her full and swollen lips.

His gaze lowered to the swell of her breasts, clearly

outlined against the soft wool of her top, the nipples hard and tempting. Too tempting for Ethan to resist as he pushed her sweater aside, before slowly lowering his head to brush his mouth against one sensitive tip, at the same time as his hand cupped her other breast and the soft pad of his thumb caressed its twin.

Encouraged by Mia's throaty groans of pleasure, he rolled her nipple between thumb and finger. Her own fingers were becoming entangled in his hair as she held him to her.

It wasn't enough—would it ever be enough with this particular woman? Would Ethan ever manage to get Mia out of his system? Out of his—

'Don't stop now, Ethan!' Mia whispered as she sensed his distraction.

He *had* to stop! Knew that he should never have started this in the first place. Not now—not here! Where Mia's father or his own mother, perhaps also unable to sleep, might walk outside at any moment and find the two of them together .

'I think you should go to bed, Mia.' He straightened her sweater before curling his fingers about her upper arms, a nerve pulsing in his tightly clenched jaw as he pushed her firmly away from him. 'Alone!'

'Ethan—'

'Believe me—you would regret this in the morning!'

Mia was breathing hard as she looked up at him in the darkness, humiliated colour heating her cheeks as he looked down at her so dispassionately. That humiliation instantly turned to anger and she wrenched out of his grasp to glare up at him. 'How can you be so cold? So unfeeling?'

'Or not,' he drawled dryly.

Mia gave him one last glowering glance before turning on her heel to run back inside the villa, closing the door decisively behind her.

Ethan watched her leave, jaw tight and his hands clenched at his sides as he fought against the desire still pounding through his body. Against the deep and primitive hunger he felt to make love to Mia until she screamed for mercy.

Fought it and lost…!

Mia had barely entered her bedroom and switched on the bedside lamp, closing the door behind her, before it was thrust open again with such force that it crashed back against the wall.

'Ethan!' she exclaimed, her eyes wide as she looked across at him where he stood silhouetted in the open doorway.

'Yes,' he ground out as he stepped into the room and closed the door behind him.

She swallowed hard. 'I— What do you want?'

He gave a humourless smile, his narrowed gaze glittering the colour of silver in the lamplight as he moved slowly across the room. 'I think it's time I showed you just how cold and unfeeling I'm *not* feeling right now!'

Mia's eyes widened even further as she watched Ethan's hands move to the bottom of his T-shirt before he lifted it up and pulled it completely over his head. He threw it down onto the carpeted floor, and her breath caught in her throat and her pulse thundered loudly in her ears as she looked at the broad expanse of his naked chest and muscled shoulders.

'Ethan, what are you doing?' she gasped breathlessly.

'What does it look like I'm doing?' He sat on the side of her bed to remove first his shoes and then his socks, before standing up again to unfasten the button on his jeans.

It looked as if Ethan was completely naked...!

'Is this cold and unfeeling enough for you?'

Five years ago Mia had thought Ethan was the most beautiful man alive, and as she looked at him now, standing with his legs slightly apart, his expression one of pure challenge, she knew it was true. A lot of men would have felt vulnerable at being so physically exposed, but not Ethan. And why should he, when his naked body bore all the perfection of a sculpture only a master in the art could have produced? Firmly muscled and yet so gracefully male, every inch of him was hard. Every single inch of him...!

Mia found herself unable to tear her gaze away from the jut of Ethan's arousal. 'What happens now, Ethan?' Her voice was so gruff with her own arousal that she could barely speak at all.

'I think that's for you to decide, don't you...?'

Mia raised her startled gaze to the hard contours of his face, those glittering silver eyes, hard cheekbones, sensuously sculptured lips.

'Me...?' she finally prompted huskily.

Ethan gave an acknowledging inclination of his head. 'I'm the one standing here naked and vulnerable. If you want me then I need you to tell me—show me—that you do.'

If Mia wanted him?

She had never wanted anything as badly as she wanted Ethan right now—could hear herself panting with that need, and knew Ethan must be able to hear it too. And yet he made no further move towards her. Just stood there naked in the middle of the bedroom, so aroused, so powerfully male he made her feel weak at the knees.

She made one last effort to resist the heated clamouring of her own body. 'If you're just here to collect on that debt you believe I owe you—'

'Forget the damned debt!' he rasped impatiently. 'I only ever said that to get some sort of response out of you.'

And it had...

'You also said we would regret it in the morning if we—if we did something like this.'

'Which only goes to prove that I occasionally talk a load of—!' He gave a slow, self-disgusted shake of his head, the darkness of his tousled hair falling across his brow. 'What I actually said was that *you* would regret it in the morning.'

He had said that, yes. Did that mean that Ethan wouldn't regret it? Or only that at this moment in time he had no interest in what the morning might bring?

Did it really matter which of those it was? Mia chided herself. Ethan was here now, in her bedroom, completely naked, with the evidence of his arousal unashamedly there for her to see.

Her gaze held his as she took a step towards him. And then another, and another. She felt encouraged by the blaze of emotion that lit his increasingly darkening eyes—until she stood in front of him and became engulfed, lost in the heated spice of his body, knowing from his tension that she only had to reach out, to touch him, for that rigid control to break.

Ethan felt on fire—as if he were burning from the inside out. Every part of him, every sensitised nerve-ending, was straining, yearning for the touch of Mia's hands. He knew that when—if—she finally touched him his control was going to break like a dam. Become a wild and unstoppable river of desire, fierce and demanding as it swept them both to the heights and the depths.

A nerve pulsed in his tightly clenched jaw as he breathed in through his nose and caught Mia's scent, like warm and salty cinnamon. His hands clenched into fists at his sides as he resisted the need to reach out and touch her, to taste her; he had told Mia it was her choice as to whether or not they took this any further, and he intended keeping to that promise. Even if the waiting was killing him by slow and agonising degrees!

She looked up at him now, through those long and silky lashes, her eyes the colour and fever-brightness of emeralds, her cheeks flushed, her lips—dear God, those lips!—swollen with desire.

Ethan could feel the bonds of his control breaking one by one, just thinking about kissing them. 'I'm coming apart here, Mia!' he warned gruffly.

Her eyes glittered up at him. 'You are?'

'Oh, yes,' he breathed raggedly.

Only to stop breathing altogether as Mia's gaze lowered and she reached out. The softness of her fingers brushed across the tip of his erection.

'Mia...' Ethan gave a strangulated groan.

Her gaze rose to meet his. 'I believe that was a yes, Ethan...'

'Thank God!' Ethan gathered her up in his arms and hungrily laid claim her mouth.

Mia wondered if the last five days—the last five years!—been leading up to this very moment. There was no room for gentleness between the two of them as they both threw off her clothes and continued to kiss, mouths hungry, hands questing, caressing, stroking, stoking the fire that blazed between them.

She lost track of time. It could have been hours, minutes, seconds later when Ethan picked her up in his arms and carried her over to the bed, lying her down against the covers before moving down beside her, over her. Mia cried out with pleasure as Ethan entered her, that pleasure spiralling out of control as she felt her orgasm explode.

Ethan allowed no time for respite from that pleasure as he wrenched his mouth from hers to kiss his way down the slope of her breast, taking Mia over that edge for a second time...

CHAPTER ELEVEN

MIA was aware of two things when she woke the following morning with the sun streaming into her bedroom window.

Firstly that Ethan was no longer in the bed. The cold sheets beside her were evidence that he must have gone some time ago.

Secondly that she felt so languidly satiated she didn't want to get up this morning. Possibly never...

Mia rolled slowly over in the bed, her breasts slightly sore and sensitive as they brushed against the sheet that covered her, reminding her of their second bout of equally heated lovemaking during the early hours of the morning.

She turned to look at the clock on the bedside table. Only seven-thirty. Why had Ethan left her so early? Why had he left at all? And where was he now...?

More to the point, how did things stand between the two of them this morning?

They hadn't spoken another word to each other after that first conversation—hadn't talked at all as they gave and received pleasure in equal measure, with only the ragged sound of their breathing to pierce the silence.

So how would they behave towards each other

now? Like the adversaries they had been yesterday? Or the lovers they had become during the night?

There was no immediate answer to that question when Mia came downstairs a short time later and found only Grace sitting at the table out on the warmth of the terrace, drinking coffee.

She looked up and gave Mia a single glance, not saying a word as she stood up to go into the kitchen, returning seconds later with another mug and the coffee pot, and placing them both down on the table close to Mia.

Mia sat down abruptly to silently pour some of the steaming hot brew into the mug, adding cream and sugar before taking a welcoming sip. She knew exactly how she must appear to the other woman, despite her attempts to brighten up her appearance with a yellow T-shirt.

Her hair had been way beyond 'bed-head' when she had looked at herself in the bathroom mirror earlier— had literally been standing up in wild tufts before Mia washed it in the shower. Her eyes were dark and heavy behind the sunglasses she had hastily pushed onto the bridge of her nose, and her lips appeared slightly swollen and puffy, as if they had been punched—or just thoroughly kissed!

'You don't look as if you slept too well last night?' Grace prompted sympathetically as she resumed her own seat at the table.

Had Mia slept at all? If she had then it had only been for a couple of hours, because it was only just after eight o'clock now, and her aching and languid body testified to the fact that she and Ethan had made love for hours...

She took another much-needed sip of coffee in order to avoid meeting Grace's concerned gaze, knowing that her hands were shaking slightly. 'I never sleep well the first night in a strange bed.'

'There's always the option of taking a siesta after lunch.' Grace wisely didn't point out that Mia hadn't actually been sleeping in a strange bed—she had been coming here to the villa since she was a child.

Another couple of sips of the reviving coffee and Mia felt able to broach the subject of the noticeable silence in the rest of the villa. 'No William or Ethan this morning?' She had meant the query to sound casually uninterested, but even to her own ears her voice sounded strained.

Where the hell was Ethan? Because until Mia had seen him again—until she had looked into his eyes—she had no idea how she was supposed to behave towards him this morning!

Grace gave a shrug. 'They've both strolled down to the bakery in the village to pick up some freshly baked croissants and pastries for our breakfast.'

Even the mention of the rich pastries caused Mia's stomach to tighten in rebellion. She knew it was Ethan she needed to see, not food.

'I'm really hoping you'll change your mind about leaving today, Mia, and stay on for a couple more days.' Grace smiled at her wistfully. 'William would so love it if you did.'

Mia's expression softened as she thought of her father. Of how good it was to see and be with him again. Their relationship might not be what it had once been, and maybe it never would be again, but perhaps with time spent together they might become easier with each other again?

Time together...

Something Mia wasn't sure, after the events of last night, she and her father could or would have. Mia had made her choices five years ago, and as a result Grace and Ethan were now her father's family; if it should turn out that last night had made things worse between herself and Ethan, rather than better, then surely it would be unfair of Mia to stay on here and become a possible cause of dissention between the three of them?

Something she and Ethan should definitely have thought of before so recklessly spending the night together!

She gave a shake of her head. 'I really only made arrangements to be away for a couple of days.'

'Surely those plans can be altered?'

'Not really.' Mia grimaced. 'I only have a staff of two, and they can't manage without me indefinitely.'

'If anyone understands a commitment to business then it's William.' Grace nodded ruefully. 'So you'll be leaving later today, as planned?'

Not knowing how things now stood between herself and Ethan…? 'Yes.'

'Then perhaps you could give some thought to spending Christmas with us?'

'Perhaps,' she echoed noncommittally, knowing that would also depend on how things stood between herself and Ethan. They could hardly all play at happy families over the holidays if she and Ethan weren't even talking to each other! 'It's still three months away.'

'I—' Grace broke off whatever it was she had been about to say to turn and smile at Ethan and William as the two men strolled around the side of the villa and out onto the terrace. The bag Ethan carried obviously contained the croissants and pastries.

A man who had spent most of the night making love had no right to look so vitally attractive the following morning, Mia decided after one guarded glance in

Ethan's direction. Everything about Ethan was compellingly male: the tight black T-shirt emphasised the raw power of his muscled chest, the denims fitted snugly over lean hips and long powerful legs. As for the way the sun shone on the darkness of his wind-tousled hair and the tanned angles of his face, reflecting off the black lenses of his wraparound sunglasses...

Making it totally impossible for Mia to look into his eyes and gauge what his mood might be this morning. As impossible as it was for Ethan to see that behind her own sunglasses her eyes were dark and heavy from lack of sleep. And uncertainty. Let's not forget the uncertainty she was feeling, Mia acknowledged self-derisively.

She swallowed down that uncertainty before turning to look at her father, pleased to see that he had more colour in his face this morning. 'Did you enjoy your walk to the village?' Mia knew the bakery in the village well— had often walked down there herself in the past, usually alone but occasionally with her father.

William gave a rueful smile. 'The doctors seem to think that a little daily exercise is good for me.'

Reminding Mia that her father had been seriously ill six months ago. Ill enough for Ethan to feel compelled to intensify the search for her, at least! 'But otherwise they've given you a clean bill of health now?'

'Oh, yes,' William assured her as he moved to sit down at the table with his wife and daughter.

All the time Mia was totally aware of the man who stood silent and distant across the terrace, but Ethan's expression was as unreadable to her as his eyes were inaccessible.

Did Ethan's body ache this morning in the same way that Mia's did? Did his legs and arms feel too heavy to move? Was he suffering from the same lack of sleep?

Did he feel the same aching need Mia did to repeat their heated lovemaking?

If he felt any of those things then it wasn't apparent as he strolled comfortably across the terrace to join them, his movements as lithe and assured as usual, with no trembling of his hands as he placed the bag of pastries on the table top, no indication of tiredness in the lightness of his voice when he spoke. 'I'll go inside and get some plates.'

This was intolerable, Mia decided shakily; if anything the atmosphere between herself and Ethan was even more tense than it had been yesterday. Not just intolerable, but unacceptable.

The two of them needed to talk. Sooner rather than later. 'I'll come and help you.' Mia stood up decisively. She wasn't the naive and trusting child she had once been, but a mature and successful woman—and she had no intention of allowing Ethan to behave as if last night had never happened!

'I think I can manage to carry four plates.'

'I—'

'Mia had just offered to make more coffee when the two of you arrived back,' Grace put in smoothly as she pushed the almost empty coffee pot towards her.

'Thanks.' Mia gave the older woman a grateful smile as she picked up the coffee pot. Her face was averted as she passed Ethan, but she was still very aware of the soft sound of his tread behind her as she went back inside the villa.

'I believe my mother was being her usual kind self just now,' Ethan rasped dryly as he followed Mia into the rustic kitchen. 'From the little I overheard of your conversation you weren't offering to make coffee at all, but discussing your arrangements for leaving later today.'

Mia put the coffee pot down before turning to look at him, her expression guarded in the pallor of her face. 'I told you from the beginning that I didn't intend to stay long.'

Ethan knew that she had. But that had been before the two of them spent the night together. Before they had made love. Twice.

His mouth thinned. 'So last night was just for old times' sake…?'

She shifted restlessly. 'I have no idea what last night was. Do you?'

Ethan had woken very early this morning, a smile curving his lips as he felt the familiar weight of Mia's head resting on his shoulder. His arm had been about her waist as he'd held her close against him, the wonderful smell of her hair permeating his senses and rousing him all over again. But a single glance at her face, at the exhaustion he'd seen beneath those relaxed features, had told him how selfish that would be. Mia needed to sleep, not make love again.

Instead he had carefully removed his arm and slid his shoulder gently from beneath her head, so as not to disturb her, lingering only long enough to take one long last look at her as she lay sleeping peacefully, before quietly letting himself out of the room to pad softly along the hallway to his own bedroom.

A long swim in the early-morning coolness of the pool had helped to dull some of his desire—and returning from the village to overhear Mia say she still intended leaving today had completely killed the rest of it!

He turned away to take the plates out of the cupboard.

'Unfinished business, probably.'

'Sorry?'

'Unfinished business,' Ethan repeated with hard dismissal as he turned to lean back against the kitchen unit. 'I believe it's perfectly natural amongst couples whose... relationships finish as abruptly as ours did five years ago.'

Mia wished she hadn't asked! That she hadn't heard Ethan dismiss last night as being so insignificant! To him, at least...

Especially when she knew that if Ethan had asked her to stay—if he had given even the smallest indication that he didn't want her to leave just yet—she would have said to hell with the coffee shop and going back to England today!

Instead of which he seemed to be saying that last night had been the end of things between them, not a new beginning...

Mia was grateful she had the shield of her sunglasses to hide the sting of tears that welled in her eyes. Tears she was determined wouldn't fall—that she couldn't let fall in front of Ethan.

She moistened dry lips before speaking. 'We didn't finish our conversation last night...'

'Which conversation would that be?' His mouth twisted. 'We didn't talk about much of anything after I came to your bedroom.'

No, they hadn't—had been too intent on making love, giving each other pleasure, to have the time or inclination to talk. 'You didn't answer my question as to whether or not my leaving five years ago was in any way responsible for your decision to stay on at Burton Industries.'

Mia had realised that earlier, as she stood beneath the stinging force of a reviving shower, thinking of the previous evening.

Just as she knew that Ethan's meteoric rise in the

management of Burton Industries was the cornerstone of the resentment she had continued to feel towards him this past five years. Take that away, and—

'I seem to recall that I told you I would have made exactly the same choices,' Ethan bit out tersely.

He had said that, yes, Mia allowed. But her head felt so befuddled this morning, from the force of their love-making and the lack of sleep, she couldn't remember now whether it had been in response to that question or another one...

'Ethan—'

'I need to take these plates out to the parents.'

'You don't think it's more important for the two of us to talk about last night?'

'Maybe later. Oh, sorry, I forgot—you won't be here later for me to talk to,' he dismissed wryly.

Mia blinked up at him. 'You won't be flying back to England when I do...?'

He shrugged. 'I've decided it would be better if I stay on here for a couple of days. In case there are any emotional repercussions for William in regard to your visit.'

Any emotional repercussions for William...

What of any emotional repercussions Mia might suffer from seeing her father again? From making love with Ethan again?

Ethan couldn't have told her any more clearly where he thought his responsibilities lay...

What had Mia expected? That last night, their incredible lovemaking, would have somehow changed things between them? That it would have blocked out the past and the long five years since they had last been together? Had she hoped that their obvious physical compatibility meant they could now find some measure of understanding between the two of them?

Ethan's easy dismissal of last night had already told her that as far as he was concerned it hadn't done any of those things...

And Mia? How did she now feel about Ethan?

The searing pain in her head, in her chest, just asking herself that question was enough for Mia to veer her thoughts sharply away from the subject; she would have plenty of time to think about that once she was back in England. Years and years in which to think. To wonder...

She drew in a ragged breath. 'I believe I'll give breakfast a miss and go upstairs and pack my things.' She needed to be alone, with time in which to lick her emotional wounds in privacy.

Ethan gave a wry smile. 'You couldn't have brought enough clothes in that small bag to need to bother!'

Mia instantly felt stung by his lack of understanding. 'Then maybe what I really need is just not to be around *you* for a while?'

His smile widened derisively. 'Now, that I can understand!'

Her frown was pained. 'Can you?'

'Oh, yes,' he drawled. 'You really should have listened to me last night when I warned you to be very sure of what you were getting yourself into.'

Yes, she should. But at the time Mia had wanted Ethan so badly she hadn't wanted to hear his warning, let alone act upon it.

And now? How did she feel about their lovemaking now?

Well, for one thing—and it was really the only thing that mattered!—Mia now realised that it couldn't actually be called making love! Without love, without that tenderness of emotion, it was just sex. And not the 'uncomplicated' kind that Ethan had once referred to so derisively, either—nothing that happened between herself and Ethan was ever uncomplicated!

'Yes, I really should have,' she conceded evenly. 'Would you make my excuses to William and Grace?' She turned abruptly on her heel to almost run towards the doorway leading into the coolness of the hallway.

'Mia!'

She came to an abrupt halt, drawing in two deep and steadying breaths before turning back to face Ethan, her heart contracting in her chest as she gazed her fill of him from behind the shield of her sunglasses, knowing she probably wouldn't see him again after today...

The expression in his eyes was as unreadable as Mia's own, and for the same reason, but there was a softening about the chiselled firmness of his mouth. 'I believe your father intends talking to you privately before you leave.'

'Oh, yes?' she said warily.

Ethan had suggested that William accompany him on the walk to the bakers earlier as a way of being alone with the older man, intending to tell William that it was time he told Mia the truth about the past. He had been preaching to the already converted, as it happened!

Grace had already had that same conversation with William in the privacy of their bedroom the evening before. Had pointed out that Mia was no longer a child in need of William's protection, and that if he wanted there to be any kind of future relationship with his daughter then it was time for him to be honest with her about the past.

'Yes.' Ethan nodded now. 'I'll be down by the pool

when—if you would like someone to talk to afterwards.' Or a shoulder to cry on!

Not that Ethan thought for one moment that Mia would choose *his* shoulder to cry on—the fact that they had spent the night together and Mia still intended leaving later today was enough of an indication that nothing had changed between them. And Ethan had never been any woman's one-night-stand! Even for old times' sake...

'Or not,' he accepted dryly when he received no response to his offer.

'Do you have any idea what he wants to talk to me about?'

'I think that's between you and William, don't you?'

She gave a frustrated shake of her head. 'Meaning that you do know but you have no intention of pre-warning me!'

Meaning that Ethan had no intention of giving Mia even more reason to dislike him! 'I'll call the air crew after breakfast and make arrangements for you to fly back to England this afternoon.'

'Fine.' She frowned. 'Thank you.'

'You're welcome,' he assured her heavily, and she gave an abrupt nod of acknowledgement before making her escape.

Which was a pretty apt description of what Mia had just done, Ethan thought; she obviously regretted their having spent the might together so much she couldn't wait to get away from him!

CHAPTER TWELVE

MIA felt as if someone had punched her in the stomach as she staggered out of her father's study just over an hour after the two of them had entered it.

As if someone had whacked her on the back of the head with a sledgehammer before dealing the final blow by kicking her legs out from under her!

She had been wrong. So very wrong.

About everything—the last four years of her parents' marriage and several years before that. Her father's supposed affair with Grace Black. Her own three-month relationship with Ethan five years ago that Mia had assumed, once she'd learnt after her mother's death and her father's relationship with Grace, had simply been Ethan using her to further his own ends.

The things Mia's father had just told her—all of it was so incredible.

Heartbreaking…

And at the same time totally believable!

How could Mia possibly have any doubts as to the truth of the things her father had told her when the telling of them had reduced her strong and dependable father to tears? Had reduced them both to tears…

No, Mia couldn't doubt her father's sincerity. Especially when she had already begun to have her own suspicions about the past since arriving here yesterday.

Ethan's revealing that he had actually once intended to teach had been a revelation, for one, and the absolute integrity Mia had sensed in those private conversations she'd had with Grace.

Grace Burton. Her father's wife. And deservedly Mia's stepmother.

Because Mia now knew everything her father had tried to protect her from all these years.

Her mother's many affairs during their marriage. The fact that Kay had been leaving them both for one of those lovers on the day of her car accident. How William had stood by the scarred and crippled mother of his young daughter after her lover had abandoned her. How that ex-lover of her mother's had then begun to blackmail him with the threat of revealing her mother's behaviour to the young and emotionally vulnerable Mia.

How William and Grace had met almost a year after Kay's accident. How they had fallen in love with each other—a love he had once again reassured Mia had nevertheless remained only a friendship until after Kay's death three years later.

Kay's suicide.

Kay *had* left William a letter, after all. A letter he had shown Mia today, which revealed how, bored and curious one day, Kay had been devastated when she'd found the evidence in a locked drawer in the desk in William's study that her previous lover had been blackmailing William ever since her car accident in order to keep his silence. It had also revealed that William knew Kay had been leaving both William and Mia at the time of the car crash...

'Are you okay?'

Mia raised startled lids to see Ethan leaning against the wall further down the hallway, looking as if he been there for some time.

Ethan. The man Mia had so mistrusted five years ago she had refused even to see him again after her mother died, cutting him out of her life as completely as she had her father.

She looked down the hallway at Ethan now, sunglasses tucked into the neck of his T-shirt, revealing those grey eyes as being both watchful and guarded.

'I thought you were going to the pool?'

'I can do that later.'

After Mia had gone back to England...

'Are you okay?' he repeated gruffly as he pushed away from the wall and walked down the hallway towards her.

Mia gave a humourless smile. 'As okay as I can be after discovering that everything I'd thought the truth was actually a lie, and everything I thought of as deception was really the truth!' she murmured self-disgustedly.

Including, she was sure, the things she had thought about her own relationship with Ethan five years ago...

Which was of absolutely no help whatsoever to Mia now!

In her pain and distrust she had accused Ethan of terrible things. Terrible and unforgivable things.

Which was why last night with Ethan had just been his way of saying goodbye. Of drawing a line under something marked 'unfinished business'...

She winced. 'Did you always know about...the things my father just told me?'

'Not initially, no,' he stated firmly. 'My mother and William explained the situation to me after your mother…died. I hope you understand that William was only trying to protect you by not sharing those things with you before now?'

'Oh, yes,' she breathed shakily.

'It's only been having you here, and both my mother and I pointing out the risk of losing you a second time, that's convinced him he had to tell you the truth now.' Ethan sighed his frustration.

She gazed up at him quizzically. 'I'm surprised you didn't feel…goaded into telling me the truth yourself this past six days?'

Ethan gave a firm shake of his head. 'I made a promise to William never to do that. My mother and I both did.'

Mia nodded. 'And I've given you every…provocation to break that promise.'

'I would never have done that,' he repeated evenly.

No, he wouldn't, Mia acknowledged heavily. Because Ethan was a man who possessed the same integrity as his mother. And that same loyalty to William. Even if his integrity and loyalty had driven a barrier between Ethan and Mia…

'Besides,' he continued, 'you've made it obvious on more than one occasion that you don't believe a word I say!'

Ethan stood in front of Mia now, close enough for her to feel the comforting heat of his body, but not close enough that he was actually touching her.

And why would he ever want to touch her again after the way Mia had behaved towards him—five years ago by disappearing without so much as a goodbye, and this last few days when she had treated him as if he were her enemy? Whatever genuine affection Ethan might once have felt for her Mia knew she had effectively killed it with her distrust and accusations.

'I owe both you and your mother an apology for the way I've behaved,' she acknowledged quietly.

That Mia was badly shaken by her conversation with her father Ethan had no doubt; it was there in the pallor of her skin, the pained darkness of her eyes, and the slight trembling of her lips that she was trying so desperatcly to keep under control.

Ethan couldn't help but admire the steady darkness of her gaze and the way she stood so straight, determined to accept his condemnation if he wanted to give it.

Something Ethan had no intention of doing. And not only because there had already been enough misunderstandings and unhappiness.

Most people would have crumbled under the barrage of information William had just shared with Mia, and she was obviously emotionally upset, but certainly not broken.

Ethan's hands slowly clenched at his sides as he resisted the impulse to reach out and take Mia in his arms, offer her comfort; her coolness towards him earlier, her quiet dignity now, told him he was the last person Mia could accept that comfort from.

'You couldn't have known.'

'I could have tricd giving you all the benefit of the doubt.' She sighed.

'William told you everything?'

'I certainly hope so; I'm not sure I can take any more shocks or surprises just now!'

No, Ethan could imagine not. It wasn't a pretty story by anyone's standards, and would certainly have shaken the very foundations of Mia's world. 'I'm just sorry you ever had to hear it at all.'

'Don't be.' Mia reached out to lightly squeeze his arm before letting her hand fall awkwardly back to her side as Ethan instantly tensed. 'I think a part of me has always known that my parents' marriage wasn't—well, that it wasn't as happy as it could have been. I've only been with Grace and William for a day and I can already see the difference in the two relationships. And once I had acknowledged that then everything else fell into place. In fact, I'm not sure that the last five years of blaming everyone and everything else for what happened weren't just some sort of self-denial on my part,' she admitted.

Ethan nodded. 'I'm not sure that I could ever have done what William did for all those years.'

But in a way he had, Mia realised. Ethan might not have known the truth until after she had disappeared five years ago, and so had been unable to tell that truth to Mia even if he had wanted to, but because of his promise to William he had chosen not to do so even when the two of them had met again the previous week—had instead suffered in silence as Mia continued to hurl her scornful accusations at him.

Ethan looked down at her searchingly now. 'And are things…easier between you and William now?'

'I'm sure that in time they will be.' Mia assured him.

'That's good.' He nodded distractedly.

'Yes.' She gave a self-conscious grimace. 'Do you have any idea where Grace is?'

'She's in the kitchen, preparing lunch. She likes to keep busy when she's worried.'

Mia drew in a ragged breath, knowing she and her reaction to the things William had intended telling her this morning were the reason for the other woman's present worry. 'I'll go and talk to her now.' She turned in the direction of the kitchen.

'Mia…?'

She turned slowly, her expression guarded. 'Yes?'

Ethan's expression was just as unreadable. 'Do you still want me to make the arrangements for you to fly back to England this afternoon?'

Did she? Mia knew she needed to spend time with her father—for the two of them to get to know each other again, for them to rebuild their relationship after so many years apart. But at the same time Mia knew that she needed some time alone first, in which to process all the things her father had told her, to come to terms with those things before they could both move forward.

And she couldn't do that around Ethan—knew that her emotions were just too confused when she was anywhere near him.

Or not…

Last night might have been Ethan's way of drawing a line under their past relationship, but it had revealed something else completely to Mia.

She was still in love with him.

She hadn't just become attracted to him all over again. Hadn't fallen in love with him all over again. She had simply never stopped loving him!

It had been five years since she'd left so abruptly, without telling anyone where she was going. One thousand eight hundred and twenty-one days, to be precise. And Mia now knew she had continued to love Ethan for every single one of them.

It was because she still loved Ethan that no other man had ever merited a second date, let alone threatened the wall Mia had built around her emotions.

She loved Ethan. Unequivocally. And she always would.

A love Ethan would never—could never—return after the way Mia had distrusted him so badly. She accepted Ethan's offer.

'I really do need to get back to the coffee shop, and my father said that he and Grace will be coming back to England themselves some time next week, anyway.'

Ethan smiled ruefully. 'If I know William, now that things are more settled between the two of you they'll be back in England some time before the end of this week, not next!'

Mia returned that smile. 'I'd like that.' Only to shift uncomfortably as Ethan just stared down at her, obviously as much at a loss as to what to say next as Mia was. 'What happened between the two of us last night—' she began.

'Am I right in assuming you would rather forget it ever happened?' he questioned knowingly.

Forget last night? Forget the pleasure Mia had found just by being in Ethan's arms again? Forget the closeness, the joy of being with him again?

Mia could never forget it.

She never wanted to forget a single moment she had spent in Ethan's company. Would no doubt spend the rest of her life haunted by those memories…

'As you said earlier, it was just unfinished business that we both needed to deal with,' she said.

It was *still* unfinished business as far as Ethan was concerned!

How could it not be when, if anything, the tension that now existed between himself and Mia was more intense than it had ever been?

'I—my father has suggested I might like to join you

all at the house in Berkshire for Christmas,' Mia spoke huskily. 'But if that's going to be a problem for you—'

'It isn't a problem for me, Mia,' Ethan bit out dismissively, his jaw clenched. 'You?'

She gave a shrug. 'No, it isn't a problem for me either.'

'That's good.'

Was it? Mia wondered painfully. Was it really 'good' that she and Ethan would meet up again in a few months' time and behave as if the two of them had only ever been polite strangers? Was that a 'good' thing?

Would it be 'good' in the years to come too, when Ethan attended those family Christmases first with his wife and then with children they had together? Would that be a 'good' thing—?'

She was getting ahead of herself! One day at a time— that was how Mia had to deal with this situation now. How she had to deal with loving Ethan...

She straightened. 'I'll go and apologise to Grace now.'

Ethan nodded abruptly. 'And I'll go and check on William.'

Mia gave a slow shake of her head. 'You've been a much better son to him than I ever was a daughter.'

He smiled. 'I doubt William would agree with that. You were, and always will be, the most important thing in his life,' Ethan said as Mia looked up at him.

'No, I believe Grace has that privilege. As she should have,' Mia added firmly, just so that there should be no more misunderstandings as to how she felt about her father's second marriage. 'Talking of which, I really should go and reassure her now...'

She looked at Ethan pointedly, knowing there was nothing left for them to say to each other, that they had already said all they needed to say. And yet knowing she didn't want this conversation with Ethan to end. She didn't want to be apart from him for even a second, let alone go back to England without him.

'Yes, you should.'

'Mmm.'

'She's been so worried about you and William.'

'Yes.'

'She'll be so happy for the two of you.'

Mia felt the now familiar sting of tears in her eyes. 'I know she will.'

And she did know.

The time for Mia's cynicism and distrust was well and truly over. Had absolutely no place in the genuine love that shone in the warmth of Grace's eyes whenever she looked at William—a love that Mia's father undoubtedly returned.

'Will four o'clock be okay?'

She blinked at Ethan. 'Sorry?'

'For your flight back to England this afternoon?'

'Oh. Yes. Four o'clock is fine.' Mia straightened, realising she had already dragged this conversation with Ethan out to an embarrassing degree.

Earning his pity would be even more painful than knowing Ethan could never return the love she felt for him. Had always felt for him.

'I'll go and offer to help Grace prepare the lunch.' Mia held her head high as she walked down the hallway to the kitchen, determined not to break down in front of Ethan.

Even if every step away from him made Mia feel as if her heart were breaking.

Grace turned and took one look at the wealth of

emotions on Mia's face as she entered the kitchen before moving forward to gather Mia into the warmth of her arms. 'You poor darling!'

'So this is goodbye.' Mia said to Ethan later that afternoon, as the two of them stood at the bottom of the steps leading up into the jet standing behind them on the tarmac.

Mia's small case was already on board, and the engines were running as it waited to take her back to England. Once again she was grateful for the shield of her sunglasses to hide how red and puffy her eyes were from the amount of crying she had done today.

Mia's emotions were so fragile at that moment that she would have preferred not to spend any more time alone with Ethan before she left, but it would have seemed churlish and ungrateful of her to refuse when he had offered to drive her to the small private airport this afternoon.

Her parting earlier from her father and Grace had been traumatic enough, but having to say goodbye to Ethan was so much worse when Mia had absolutely no idea when or if she would see him again!

Especially so after Ethan had seemed so politely distant on the drive here…

'For now.' He nodded abruptly.

Mia blinked. 'I— Yes.' She attempted a smile. 'I'm sure there will be lots of family occasions when we'll have to be polite to each other for the sake of the parents, at least.'

Mia couldn't have told Ethan any more clearly than that just how much of a trial she was going to find those occasions!

His mouth tightened. 'I'll try to keep them to a minimum.'

'I—thank you.' She gave a pained frown.

Ethan bit back his impatience. 'No problem. Do you have everything you need for the flight?'

'I only brought my case and bag—oh, I almost forgot to give you these!' She began to rummage through the contents of her large shoulder bag to produce a square box that she held out to him. 'I…I was economical with the truth yesterday, when I said I hadn't brought any with me…'

Ethan slowly took the box of cookies from her. 'Economical with the truth…?'

'Okay—I outright lied,' Mia acknowledged.

He frowned as he looked down at the box he now held.

'Why?'

She shrugged. 'I think I was just being difficult.'

'Because I was the one to ask you about the cookies?'

Mia shifted uncomfortably. 'Probably.'

His frown deepened. 'Do you dislike me so much that you had to lie about something so trivial?'

'Of course I don't dislike—' She abruptly broke off the fierce denial. 'I don't dislike you, Ethan,' she repeated evenly.

'I disagree. You may have forgiven William for keeping the truth from you all those years, but you haven't forgiven me, have you?' It was more a statement than a question.

'Don't be silly, Ethan,' Mia dismissed awkwardly.

Was it 'silly' of Ethan to know that Mia had avoided his company completely following their conversation this morning in the hallway outside her father's study?

Was it 'silly' of him to feel the distance that now yawned between the two of them? Was it 'silly' of him to realise from Mia's silence that having him drive her to the airport was the last thing she had wanted? Was it 'silly' of him to know that Mia couldn't wait to get on the plane and fly back to England?

And to realise that the reason she felt that way was because more than anything else she wanted to get away from *him*...

Ethan had no idea what he had expected once William had told Mia the truth, but it certainly wasn't this—this complete estrangement between himself and Mia! He had thought—had hoped—that her knowing the truth at last might make things easier for the two of them. That they might at least become friends.

'Ethan...?'

He focused on her with effort, a nerve pulsing in his clenched jaw as he saw the puzzlement in her face as she looked up at him. 'I guess this really is goodbye, then?' he said.

'Until Christmas,' she agreed brightly.

Christmas? How long away was Christmas? Months, damn it. 'Maybe we'll meet up at the parents' before then?'

'Maybe.' But she didn't look too enthusiastic about the possibility. 'I really do have to go, Ethan.' She glanced up the steps of the plane to where Karen stood waiting to welcome her on board.

Ethan stepped back stiffly, totally aware of the invisible wall about Mia that said *don't come any nearer.* 'Have a good flight.'

She nodded abruptly. 'And you take care driving back to the villa.'

Ethan stood and watched as Mia climbed the steps

up into the plane. Saw the way she smiled at the warmly welcoming Karen before she disappeared inside the plane without sparing Ethan so much as a second glance.

CHAPTER THIRTEEN

'MIND if I join you?'

Unlike the last time this had happened, eight weeks ago, Mia had absolutely no doubt it was Ethan talking to her this time, as she sat in one of the booths at the coffee shop taking her afternoon break.

It had been a long six weeks as far as Mia was concerned, when the only news she'd had of Ethan came from the regular visits she now paid to Grace and William's home in Berkshire. As Ethan had predicted, the older couple had returned from the South of France only days after Mia, and she had driven out to have dinner with them the following evening. She had continued to have dinner with the two of them at least twice a week since.

And Ethan hadn't been present on a single one of those occasions.

Mia could only presume that absence to have been deliberate on his part. Which made his being here at the coffee shop now all the more surprising...

Mia schooled her features before looking up at him, hoping that the hungry need she felt at just being able to gaze her fill of him again wasn't too obvious!

Ethan looked wonderful, but tired, Mia thought as her gaze became searching on the grim tension of his face. He also looked as if he had lost weight this past six weeks...

The fact that he wore one of those dark and perfectly tailored suits with a formal silk shirt and meticulously knotted tie was testament to the fact that Ethan had obviously come here straight from his office, and yet he somehow still managed to look less—less *kempt* than he had when Mia had last seen him seven weeks ago. His hair looked as if it was in need of a trim as it curled over the collar of his shirt, and there were dark shadows under his eyes and grim lines beside his mouth. Both those things were emphasised by the fact that his face seemed thinner, leaner, those sculptured cheekbones more prominent beneath the hollows of his eyes.

Mia forced a bright smile. 'You look as if you need one of my triple chocolate cookies!'

Ethan was well aware of how he looked. Just as he was aware that in contrast to his own drawn appearance Mia looked glowing in a fitted black sweater and low-rider black denims. Positively glowing. Her eyes shone deeply green, her cheeks were tinged with a becoming flush and no longer as hollow as they had been, and her smile was one of complete ease.

What had Ethan expected? He knew from his conversations with his mother that Mia visited the older couple often now—comfortable and happy visits that were becoming easier all the time. The two women were even intending to go Christmas shopping on Mia's next day off.

He glanced around the almost empty coffee shop. 'Not so busy today?'

'The lull before the after-school storm,' she said lightly. 'Can I tempt you with a coffee and a cookie? On the house,' she added teasingly.

Ethan shook his head. 'If you're not too busy I would rather go somewhere we can talk privately.'

Mia tensed. 'There's nothing wrong, is there? My father and Grace—?'

'Were both fine when I had lunch with them earlier today,' he reassured her. 'And, no, Mia, this is just me wanting to talk to you.'

Mia's heart gave a leap in her chest. Before common sense took over. Ethan hadn't wanted to see her on his own behalf for the last six weeks. There was absolutely no reason to suppose his visit today was of a personal nature either. There was certainly nothing in the grimness of his expression to indicate he had longed as desperately to see her again as she had him!

'It's a little cold to go to the park today,' she said, the temperature outside having dropped to single figures the last few days. 'But we could go upstairs to my apartment?'

'Fine.' Ethan's tense nod wasn't in the least encouraging.

Dee raised knowing brows as Mia walked past the counter, before her eager gaze quickly passed on to the broodingly handsome Ethan as he followed Mia down the hallway to the stairs leading up to her apartment. No doubt Mia's young assistant imagined the two of them were going upstairs for a romantic tryst!

If only…!

'So.' Mia's hands were tightly gripped together as she turned to face Ethan once they were upstairs in the comfort of her sitting room, Mia having ignited the gas beneath the log fire to give the room an extra glow. 'What can I do for you, Ethan?'

'May I?' Ethan waited for her nod of assent before slipping off his overcoat and laying it over the back of one of the chairs, his grey gaze enigmatic as he looked across at her. 'How have you been?'

How had Mia *been*?

Emotionally? Extremely lonely. The sort of deep and aching loneliness that persisted even in the midst of a crowd. Even when Mia was busy at work, or when she visited Grace and William and felt surrounded by the warmth of their love.

Because it wasn't Ethan she was with. And it wasn't Ethan's love that surrounded her.

But otherwise? Her relationship with her father and Grace was blossoming. The coffee shop was still amazingly busy. And she was healthy. Very much so, in fact…

'I'm doing well, thanks. You?'

He shrugged as he pushed his hands into the pockets of his trousers. 'Keeping busy.' He nodded abruptly. 'I—do you think I might have that coffee after all…?'

'Of course.' Mia was relieved to have something to do.

Although she was a little less certain of that when Ethan followed her out to the kitchen and stood in the doorway, watching her as she moved self-consciously around the small confines of the room preparing the coffee, placing several triple chocolate cookies on a plate too, before picking up the tray to carry it back into the sitting room.

'Here—let me.'

Mia gave a start as she realised that Ethan had moved silently across the kitchen to stand beside her, was taking the laden tray away from her now. The leanness of his fingers brushed lightly against hers—enough to cause a shiver of awareness down the length of her spine.

That quiver deepened as she briefly felt the warmth

of his body so close to her own, but Ethan was obviously completely unaffected as he turned away abruptly to carry to tray through to the sitting room.

Mia drew in a deep and controlling breath before slowly following him, still uncertain as to what Ethan was actually doing here.

He satisfied that curiosity as Mia sat on the couch to pour the coffee. 'I thought that we ought to talk about Christmas.'

Mia eyed him uncertainly as he stood beside the glowing fireplace. 'Christmas…?'

'Yes.' Ethan sighed. 'We talked about it briefly while we were in the South of France, and I thought we had agreed—Mia, I know you've been avoiding me the past six weeks, and I can understand why that is, but—'

'I've been avoiding *you*?' she cut in incredulously, before her expression sharpened. 'What do you mean you understand why that is?'

He gave another shrug. 'I appreciate that you probably feel a little…awkward being around me again after we spent the night together.'

That was one way of describing how Mia regarded the night they had made love and slept together six weeks ago!

'And?' she prompted.

'And I'm not here to put any pressure on you to see or be with me again. I just think it would be better for the parents if we could talk about Christmas.' He began to pace restlessly. 'I know they want both of us to be with them for the holidays, and the way things are between the two of us at the moment that's going to be very difficult. For all of us.'

Christmas was still five weeks away, but Mia had already accepted Grace and William's invitation to stay with them. After years of spending Christmas on her own, she was very much looking forward to being with her family.

All her family…

Another reason for Mia to accept the parents' invitation had been because she was sure Ethan would have to make an appearance some time during the Christmas period…

She moistened slightly numbed lips before speaking. 'You would rather I didn't go to Berkshire for Christmas?'

'No, of course not!' Ethan protested impatiently. 'If the two of us can't come to some sort of an understanding then I'll be the one to make other arrangements.'

Mia frowned as she slowly handed him one of the two mugs of coffee she had just poured. 'Such as…?'

He shrugged. 'I can always tell the parents I've decided I'm going skiing this year.'

'And are you?'

'I'm really hoping not.' Ethan grimaced before sipping his coffee. 'Believe it or not, these past few years I've actually come to like and appreciate family Christmases.'

Mia did believe him—had no doubt that the years he and Grace had spent Christmas on their own, although a happy time for them, still wouldn't have had the warmth of the real family Christmases they'd had with William the last four years.

She gave a shaky sigh. 'Then it's me you have a problem being with?' Her heart sank at the very thought of having Ethan so disinclined to spend time in her company he was even considering turning down the invitation to spend Christmas with their parents.

Ethan didn't have a problem being with Mia at all! Well…no more of a problem than he'd ever had…

He put his coffee mug down on the table before distractedly picking up one of the triple chocolate biscuits from the plate and taking a bite. His senses were immediately assailed by the delight of eating one of Mia's unique-tasting cookies.

The box Mia had handed him at the airport that last afternoon in the South of France sat alone and unopened in the kitchen of Ethan's apartment. A silent and constant reminder of the woman who had baked them…

The cookie he was eating turned to sawdust in his mouth, and he put it down on the plate mainly uneaten before straightening determinedly. 'I'm not the one who expressed a definite wish not to see you this past six weeks.'

Mia looked up at him blankly. 'Sorry…?'

Ethan breathed impatiently. 'I'm not criticising you for feeling the way you do, Mia; I've already told you I completely understand why it is you feel that way. I'm just hoping we can talk this through and—'

'Come to an understanding,' Mia finished with another frown. 'Ethan, I haven't expressed a wish—definite or otherwise—not to see you since we all came back from the South of France…'

He looked puzzled. 'But—my mother said—'

'Yes?'

Ethan felt slightly dazed as he looked down at her. 'I've been spending time with my mother and William specifically on the evenings you weren't going to be there.'

'I'm well aware of that.' Mia sighed.

'Because my mother told me that was the way you preferred it…'

'Grace did…?' Mia looked even more bewildered.

Ethan became very still, his thoughts racing with the possibilities of this conversation. And, no matter what direction he approached the problem from, it all came back to his mother having told him that Mia would prefer not see him at the moment.

'Oh, hell…!' Ethan groaned as he dropped down onto the sofa beside Mia. 'I've been played, Mia,' he muttered disgustedly. 'And by my own mother, damn it!'

'I don't understand.'

No, she probably didn't, Ethan appreciated. Mia knew him well—very well in some circumstances—but his mother appeared to know him better than even Ethan had realised.

He pinched the bridge of his nose to ease his tension before glancing across at Mia. Who still looked totally confused. Ethan gave her a rueful smile. 'My mother has been using a little reverse psychology. Telling me you didn't want to see me and no doubt allowing *you* to believe I didn't want to see you either…?'

'Yes!' Mia gasped softly as she stood up restlessly. 'But why would she do such a thing?' She gave a disbelieving shake of her head.

Ethan gave an affectionate grimace. 'In the expectation that I would eventually break and do exactly as I've done! That I would come here, Mia,' he explained.

Mia had come to know Grace well enough this past six weeks to know that the other woman didn't have a vindictive bone in her body. That William and their family were the most important things in her life. Which made Ethan's conviction that his mother had deliberately kept them apart all the harder to comprehend…

Ethan sighed deeply. 'I'll have a talk with her.'

'And say what?' Mia still had absolutely no idea what was going on!

'That she's mistaken.'

'Ethan—'

'My mother is under the misapprehension that the two of us—' Ethan gave a shake of his head. 'Mia, she's been playing matchmaker.'

'Matchmaker?' Mia echoed forcefully. 'Between the two of us?'

Ethan nodded grimly. 'Unbelievable—but true, I'm afraid.'

Mia couldn't have agreed more. Grace knew Ethan better than anyone. She couldn't possibly believe that he—?

Mia had believed she and Grace had become friends these past few weeks—certainly close enough friends for Grace to have realized—

Grace *did* know Ethan better than anyone else. And Mia wasn't mistaken; she and Grace *had* definitely become friends this past six weeks.

What had Grace said to her in the kitchen during that strange conversation the evening Mia had arrived in the South of France? That Mia had been one of her brightest pupils but lacking in emotional insight. The older woman had also said later that Mia needed to open her eyes to the truth that was right under her nose if she cared to look for it…

Mia eyed Ethan searchingly now. 'Why do you think she did that…?'

He gave a derisive smile. 'These last few weeks she's begun to mention her wish to have grandchildren one day.'

'Grandchildren…?' Mia desperately tried to keep her balance as the room suddenly began to tilt and sway.

Tried and failed.

As she did in her effort to grasp hold of the mantelpiece as she felt herself pitching forward towards the fire—before she knew no more and total blackness washed over her.

'Mia? For God's sake, Mia! Mia—'

'I'm okay, Ethan,' she managed to breathe weakly, keeping her eyes closed as she felt the gentleness of his fingers brushing against the hair at her temples and tried to work out exactly where she was.

Lying on the sofa, by the feel of it. And nothing hurt—not her head, or when she flexed her arms and legs—so she'd probably avoided making contact with the fireplace after all.

'Damn it, Mia, what the hell happened?' Ethan's voice was very close and slightly above her, one of her hands clasped tightly in his much larger one as he sat on the edge of the sofa beside her.

She had fainted—that was what had happened.

She had heard Ethan say Grace wished to have grandchildren and then fainted...

'Can I get you anything?' Ethan prompted worriedly. 'Some water? Tea—'

'No tea.' Mia groaned in protest as she finally opened her eyes to look up and see Ethan's concerned face looming darkly above her. 'Could you just...back off a little?' She blinked as she tried to focus.

Ethan scowled as he stood up abruptly; Mia couldn't have told him any more clearly that she found his close proximity unacceptable.

'Maybe I should go—'

'No!' Mia's immediate protest was accompanied by her trying to sit up.

'Mia, are you ill?' Ethan prompted concernedly, once she was sitting up with her back pressed against the sofa, her cheeks having a slightly green tinge to them.

'No.' She gave a weak smile. 'You were saying something about your mother wanting grandchildren…?' she reminded him.

Ethan gave an impatient shake of his head. 'That isn't important right now.' He was still totally consumed with the image of Mia pitching headfirst towards the gas fire. Only his quick reflexes had stopped that from happening as he had managed to scoop her up in his arms.

'Ethan, what does Grace's having deliberately kept the two of us apart the past six weeks have to do with her wanting grandchildren?'

Ethan frowned his irritation, knowing he was still too rattled by Mia's having fainted to be able to prevaricate. 'I believe she's realised that getting the two of us together is the only way I'm ever going to provide her with any!'

Mia became very still. 'Would you care to explain that remark?'

'Not particularly,' Ethan grated. 'But I will—if you insist…?' he added heavily as Mia continued to look up at him.

She moistened her lips with the tip of her tongue. 'I do, yes.'

'I thought you might,' Ethan muttered. 'When you left five years ago—'

'When I disappeared?' she corrected.

'Yes,' he acknowledged gruffly. 'Mia, remember you once asked me if I had bothered to look for you?' He waited for her nod of confirmation before continuing. 'I looked—okay? For days, weeks, months. I was as obsessed—more obsessed with finding you than your father was. I was the one who visited your old school-friends. People I thought might know you from university. Anyone who might have the least idea of where you had gone. And a lot of people who didn't,' he added harshly.

'Why...?' she breathed softly.

His eyes glittered pale silver. 'Because I was in love with you!'

Mia drew in a sharp breath. 'You...?'

'Yes.' Ethan looked at her stunned expression. 'I was totally, irrevocably in love with the boss's daughter! And when you left the way you did, without so much as a goodbye—'

'You were in love with me?' Mia repeated sharply.

'Of course I was in love with you!' He glared his impatience. 'Damn it, Mia, anyone who knew me—my mother for one, obviously—' he added self-derisively, 'could have told you how I felt. That the way I was with you was unprecedented. I had dated a lot at university, but never exclusively. And never, *ever* to the point that I spent my every waking moment—and most of my sleeping ones too!—with the same woman for three months.'

'I never knew...'

'That I couldn't get enough of you? That I ensured we were together day and night because any moment I wasn't with you seemed like wasted time to me—an agony of loneliness that disappeared the moment I was with you again?'

The same aching loneliness Mia had known this past six weeks...

'You never told me you felt that way about me,' she breathed dazedly.

'Because I was dating the boss's daughter!' Ethan

repeated. 'Damn it, I *knew* how it looked. What people would assume—say about me. What *you* said about me,' he added.

She shook her head. 'I was still angry and hurt when I said those things to you—'

'That doesn't mean you didn't believe them.' He sighed. 'That others didn't believe it, too.'

'I'm not interested in what other people did or didn't think.'

'I was,' Ethan bit out tautly. 'But I put up with the knowing looks, the whispered conversations at Burton Industries that would stop the moment I entered a room. I put up with it because the alternative—not being with you— was unthinkable.'

Mia stood up abruptly, taking several seconds to regain her balance as the room began to tilt again. 'Why did you never tell me any of these things, Ethan?' She looked at him beseechingly. 'Why didn't you share those things with me?'

'Because I was scared, damn it! I've never been so scared. I thought if I told you about the rumours and speculation you might start to think they could be true.' He groaned hoarsely. 'My God, Mia, you were everything to me! At the time I would have sold my soul to the devil to keep you.'

At the time... Before Mia had completely ruined everything by treating Ethan with the same distrust and contempt as everyone else obviously had because he was dating the boss's daughter...!

Ethan gave a shake of his head. 'I thought if I gave you time to fall in love with me that eventually none of those things would matter. That we could get married and—'

'You wanted to marry me?' Mia gasped weakly.

He nodded. 'Enough to put up with gossip and innuendo for the rest of my life if I had to. As it turned out, I didn't have to.'

Mia had never known any of this. Had been so deeply in love with Ethan that she hadn't looked beyond their relationship—hadn't even thought of what others might think of him because he was dating William Burton's daughter. That had come later. Once Mia had learnt of William's involvement with Grace. After which she had made exactly those same accusations...

'And now...?'

Ethan gave a dismissive shrug. 'Now I'm just trying to establish enough of...of an understanding between the two of us to allow my mother and William to have something resembling a normal family.'

Mia chewed on her bottom lip. 'I see.'

'Somehow I doubt that,' Ethan drawled. 'But in the circumstances it's the best I can do.'

Mia gave a pained frown. 'Could I—could I just—in my own defence could I just say that I was in love with you too five years ago?'

What Ethan would have given to have Mia say that at the time! Nothing else would have mattered. Not the gossip. The innuendos. He would certainly never have accepted her refusals to see him again after her mother's funeral—would have kicked down a few doors to get to her if he'd had to. Would have made her believe in him. Trust him.

As it was, it was all five years too late...

He swallowed hard. 'I'm glad we've finally had this conversation, Mia,' he assured her. 'I'm just not sure where we go from here.'

'Where would you like us to go?' Mia prompted quietly.

Ethan dropped down into one of the armchairs. 'Hell if I know!'

Mia looked down at him, still stunned at knowing Ethan had been in love with her all those years ago, but knowing she had to get by that—had to concentrate on the here and now if they were to have any sort of future. Even if Ethan only wanted them to become friends for the sake of their parents...

She drew in a ragged breath. 'I was extremely young five years ago, Ethan,' she acknowledged ruefully. 'Too young and naive to even realise how you felt about me, and I—I'm sorry for that.' She owed Ethan that much, at least. 'If it's any consolation, for me the last five years have been...hell,' she concluded flatly.

'Despite everything you missed your father?' Ethan murmured understandingly.

'Oh, yes,' Mia admitted shakily. 'I was so tempted to come back when I saw the announcement in the newspapers of his having had a heart attack. But I didn't.' She gave a self-disgusted shake of her head. 'Because I was scared too, Ethan. Not only of seeing my father and Grace again, but of seeing *you*.'

Mia had had lots of time to think this past six weeks— to recognise and acknowledge why she had behaved in the way that she had. And all of it came back to her being in love with Ethan...

'Those photographs!' Ethan's face was pale. 'I was physically sick too after seeing them. The thought that it might be you...' He gave a shake of his head. 'I lived through the same hell as William for that twenty-four hours while we waited for pathology reports and dental records to be verified.'

Mia could barely breathe. 'You did...?' That had only been eight months ago...

'Hell, yes!' His grey eyes were once again a glittering silver as he glared up at her. 'To think that that body might possibly be the woman I had once loved…!' He shook his head again. 'Sick doesn't even *begin* to describe how I felt!'

The woman Ethan had once loved…

Past tense.

But not for Mia…

'Ethan, I didn't just miss my father for those five years.' Her gaze was very steady on his. 'I missed you more than I missed anyone or anything!' She gave a self-conscious laugh as Ethan looked stunned by the admission. 'I haven't dated very often this past five years, but the dates I have had,' she continued firmly, as Ethan scowled, 'have been…disastrous. Because none of those men were you. And I—I so very much needed them to be you!'

Ethan could barely breathe. 'You did?'

'Oh, yes.' Mia gave a choked laugh. 'I've never been even remotely in danger of falling in love with anyone else. Never so much as been on a second date with the same man, let alone gone to bed with him—' She broke off as Ethan surged restlessly to his feet, but held her ground as he came forcefully towards her, determined to finish what she had started. 'Ethan, after all that you've said today I—I owe you this much in return. The truth is, Ethan, I've never stopped loving you. Not even for a moment.'

Ethan looked down at her searchingly, seeing the evidence of that love shining in the deep green depths of her eyes and the emotional trembling of her lips. 'You still love me…?' he finally breathed hesitantly.

She gave a tremulous smile. 'Always.'

Ethan could barely breathe as he reached out to lightly

clasp the tops of her arms. 'But you left me again after we'd made love in the South of France...'

'Because when I woke up and found you gone I thought you regretted it.'

'And that's the reason you went ahead with you decision to leave that afternoon?' He groaned disbelievingly.

'Yes.'

'I could never regret making love with you, Mia!' he stated firmly. 'Ever. Not even for a moment. I love you. I always have. I always will!' he vowed fiercely. 'I thought *you* regretted it.'

A sob caught in her throat as she buried her face against his chest. 'I can't believe we've both been so foolish!'

'But no more,' Ethan said as he held her tightly against him, his cheek resting on the silkiness of her hair. 'Marry me, Mia. Marry me and make me the happiest man alive!'

The love she felt for him glowed in her eyes as she looked up at him. 'Any time. Anywhere,' she whispered as Ethan's mouth claimed hers.

'If it's okay with you, I would prefer that we don't wait too long to get married, Mia,' Ethan told her warmly a long time later, as the two of them lay naked and entwined in Mia's bed. 'I love you, you love me, and we've been apart long enough already.'

Mia smiled contentedly, knowing she would never tire of hearing Ethan tell her that he loved her—as she would never tire of telling him how much she loved him. 'And no doubt my father and Grace would like it if the two of us were married before their first grandchild's born.'

'No doubt.' Ethan lay relaxed and satiated beside her, totally content, happy in a way he could never remember being before.

'Which should be in about seven and a half months' time...'

Mia held her breath as she waited for Ethan's reaction to hearing he was going to be a father. Not that she had any doubt now how much and for how long he had loved her—she just knew it was going to be something of a shock to learn that he was also going to be a father.

Mia hadn't known what to make of her symptoms at first—the extreme tiredness, the sudden feeling of nausea at the smell of tea—until she had also realised that she had missed a period.

Her hands had been shaking when she'd used the pregnancy test she had hurried out to buy, before a feeling of extreme calm and euphoric happiness had come over her when she'd seen that tell-tale blue line across the tiny screen and known that she was pregnant with Ethan's baby. That no matter what she would always have a tiny part of him to love and cherish for ever.

The fact that the two of them loved each other after all, and were going to be married, increased that happiness a hundred—a thousandfold!

'Ethan?' she prompted, as she moved up on her elbows to look at him. His eyes were wide with shock, his face white against the cream pillows. 'Ethan...?' she repeated hesitantly. 'Don't you want this baby...?'

'Want it?' he repeated fiercely as he rolled over to push her gently back against the pillows. 'I want it so badly I can't even begin to tell you how much...!' His wondering gaze travelled down to her stomach. 'Really...?' His hand curved over the tiny swell.

'Really,' she confirmed happily. 'Another week of not

seeing you and I was going to hunt you down and tell you,' she added ruefully.

Ethan's gaze was adoring on the flushed beauty of her face. 'All that talk about grandchildren...do you think my mother knows?'

'I wouldn't be at all surprised,' Mia murmured happily as she entwined her arms about his neck.

Ethan gave al shake of his head. 'Never underestimate mothers!'

'As someone who will shortly become one, I wholeheartedly agree!'

'You *are* pleased about the baby? Oh, God—not just you but a baby too...!' He trembled slightly. 'I don't deserve to be this happy,' he choked as he buried his face against the softness of her throat.

'You deserve this and more.' Mia's arms tightened about him. 'I was such an idiot for so long,' she added heavily. 'I'm the one who doesn't deserve any of this!'

Ethan raised his head. 'You're talking about the woman I love,' he drawled chidingly.

'The idiot you love,' she corrected self-disgustedly. 'Are you really all right with this, Ethan?' She looked up at him frowningly. 'What about the dream you had of becoming a teacher? With the baby and the coffee shop I can hardly offer to even try and take over at Burton Industries...'

Ethan gave a husky laugh. 'I'm perfectly happy running Burton Industries. Even more so now that I know our children will one day inherit it,' he added soberly. 'Besides which, as CEO of Burton Industries, I've been a guest lecturer at LSE for the past two years.' He shrugged dismissively. 'It's enough. As long as I have you, Mia, and any children that come along in the future, I'll be happy.'

Mia didn't doubt that Ethan meant every word he said—could see the truth of it as he gazed down at her with absolute love in his eyes.

'I love you so much, Ethan,' she breathed.

'And I love you, Mia.'

Ethan was right—it was enough…

CLASSIC

Quintessential, modern love stories
that are romance at its finest.

COMING NEXT MONTH from Harlequin Presents® EXTRA
AVAILABLE JANUARY 10, 2012

**#181 IN A STORM OF
SCANDAL**
Irresistible Italians
Kim Lawrence

**#182 A DANGEROUS
INFATUATION**
Irresistible Italians
Chantelle Shaw

**#183 WORKING WITH THE
ENEMY**
Risky Business
Susan Stephens

**#184 THERE'S SOMETHING
ABOUT A REBEL...**
Risky Business
Anne Oliver

COMING NEXT MONTH from Harlequin Presents®
AVAILABLE JANUARY 31, 2012

**#3041 MONARCH OF THE
SANDS**
Sharon Kendrick

#3042 THE LONE WOLFE
The Notorious Wolfes
Kate Hewitt

**#3043 ONCE A FERRARA
WIFE...**
Sarah Morgan

**#3044 PRINCESS FROM
THE PAST**
Caitlin Crews

**#3045 FIANCÉE FOR
ONE NIGHT**
21st Century Bosses
Trish Morey

**#3046 THE PETROV
PROPOSAL**
Maisey Yates

You can find more information on upcoming Harlequin® titles,
free excerpts and more at www.HarlequinInsideRomance.com.

HPCNM0112

REQUEST YOUR FREE BOOKS!

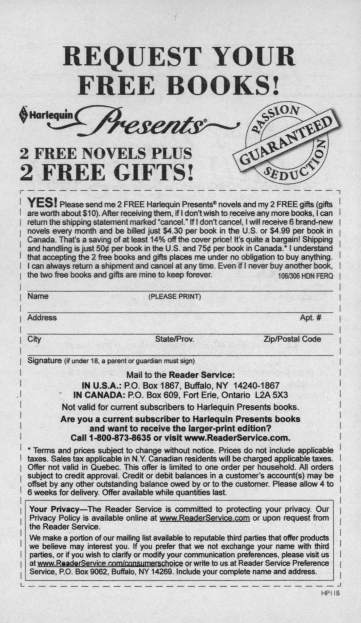

♦Harlequin *Presents*

PASSION GUARANTEED SEDUCTION

2 FREE NOVELS PLUS
2 FREE GIFTS!

YES! Please send me 2 FREE Harlequin Presents® novels and my 2 FREE gifts (gifts are worth about $10). After receiving them, if I don't wish to receive any more books, I can return the shipping statement marked "cancel." If I don't cancel, I will receive 6 brand-new novels every month and be billed just $4.30 per book in the U.S. or $4.99 per book in Canada. That's a saving of at least 14% off the cover price! It's quite a bargain! Shipping and handling is just 50¢ per book in the U.S. and 75¢ per book in Canada.* I understand that accepting the 2 free books and gifts places me under no obligation to buy anything. I can always return a shipment and cancel at any time. Even if I never buy another book, the two free books and gifts are mine to keep forever.

106/306 HDN FERQ

Name	(PLEASE PRINT)	
Address		Apt. #
City	State/Prov.	Zip/Postal Code

Signature (if under 18, a parent or guardian must sign)

Mail to the Reader Service:
IN U.S.A.: P.O. Box 1867, Buffalo, NY 14240-1867
IN CANADA: P.O. Box 609, Fort Erie, Ontario L2A 5X3

Not valid for current subscribers to Harlequin Presents books.

**Are you a current subscriber to Harlequin Presents books
and want to receive the larger-print edition?
Call 1-800-873-8635 or visit www.ReaderService.com.**

* Terms and prices subject to change without notice. Prices do not include applicable taxes. Sales tax applicable in N.Y. Canadian residents will be charged applicable taxes. Offer not valid in Quebec. This offer is limited to one order per household. All orders subject to credit approval. Credit or debit balances in a customer's account(s) may be offset by any other outstanding balance owed by or to the customer. Please allow 4 to 6 weeks for delivery. Offer available while quantities last.

Your Privacy—The Reader Service is committed to protecting your privacy. Our Privacy Policy is available online at www.ReaderService.com or upon request from the Reader Service.

We make a portion of our mailing list available to reputable third parties that offer products we believe may interest you. If you prefer that we not exchange your name with third parties, or if you wish to clarify or modify your communication preferences, please visit us at www.ReaderService.com/consumerschoice or write to us at Reader Service Preference Service, P.O. Box 9062, Buffalo, NY 14269. Include your complete name and address.

HPI1B

USA TODAY bestselling author

Sarah Morgan

brings readers another enchanting story

ONCE A FERRARA WIFE...

When Laurel Ferrara is summoned back to Sicily
by her estranged husband, billionaire
Cristiano Ferrara, Laurel knows things are about
to heat up. And Cristiano's power is a potent
reminder of his Sicilian dynasty's unbreakable rule:
once a Ferrara wife, always a Ferrara wife....

Sparks fly this February

*Louisa Morgan loves being around children.
So when she has the opportunity to tutor bedridden Ellie,
she's determined to bring joy back into the motherless
girl's world. Can she also help Ellie's father open his
heart again? Read on for a sneak peek of*

THE COWBOY FATHER

*by Linda Ford,
available February 2012 from Love Inspired Historical.*

Why had Louisa thought she could do this job? A bubble of self-pity whispered she was totally useless, but Louisa ignored it. She wasn't useless. She could help Ellie if the child allowed it.

Emmet walked her out, waiting until they were out of earshot to speak. "I sense you and Ellie are not getting along."

"Ellie has lost her freedom. On top of that, everything is new. Familiar things are gone. Her only defense is to exert what little independence she has left. I believe she will soon tire of it and find there are more enjoyable ways to pass the time."

He looked doubtful. Louisa feared he would tell her not to return. But after several seconds' consideration, he sighed heavily. "You're right about one thing. She's lost everything. She can hardly be blamed for feeling out of sorts."

"She hasn't lost everything, though." Her words were quiet, coming from a place full of certainty that Emmet was more than enough for this child. "She has you."

"She'll always have me. As long as I live." He clenched his fists. "And I fully intend to raise her in such a way that even if something happened to me, she would never feel like I was gone. I'd be in her thoughts and in her actions every day."

Peace filled Louisa. "Exactly what my father did."

Their gazes connected, forged a single thought about fathers and daughters…how each needed the other. How sweet the relationship was.

Louisa tipped her head away first. "I'll see you tomorrow."

Emmet nodded. "Until tomorrow then."

She climbed behind the wheel of their automobile and turned toward home. She admired Emmet's devotion to his child. It reminded her of the love her own father had lavished on Louisa and her sisters. Louisa smiled as fond memories of her father filled her thoughts. Ellie was a fortunate child to know such love.

Louisa understands what both father and daughter are going through. Will her compassion help them heal—and form a new family? Find out in
THE COWBOY FATHER
by Linda Ford, available February 14, 2012.

Love Inspired Books celebrates 15 years of inspirational romance in 2012! February puts the spotlight on Love Inspired Historical, with each book celebrating family and the special place it has in our hearts. Be sure to pick up all four Love Inspired Historical stories, available February 14, wherever books are sold.

Harlequin Super Romance

Discover a touching new trilogy from
USA TODAY bestselling author

Janice Kay Johnson

Between Love and Duty

As the eldest brother of three, Duncan MacLachlan
is used to being in control and maintaining an
emotional distance; as a police captain it's his job.
But when he meets Jane Brooks, Duncan soon finds
his control slipping away. Together, they fight for a
young boy's future, and soon Duncan finds himself
hoping to build a future with Jane.

Available February 2012

From Father to Son
(March 2012)

The Call of Bravery
(April 2012)